Event Horizon

Chances Are Series

Book 1

TINA PROFFITT

All Rights Reserved 2017

Event Horizon

I wrote this one for both of us.

This book is a work of fiction.
Any similarities to persons living or dead are purely coincidental.

Chapter 1

Not now!

Why did he have to be at work when the unspeakable happened?

Annie tucked a chunk of her reddish brown hair behind her ear and listened to the phone in her hand. It rang and rang. No answer. Looking down at fingers that shook, all she saw were the scars.

"Is this Annabel Peters Morgan?" the doctor had said only minutes before.

"Yes, this is Annie."

"I found your number in your mother's phone. I'm afraid I've got bad news."

Now the phone in her hand went to voice mail. She looked at it as if it could tell her where her husband was.

"Hi, you've reached Chance Morgan. If you'd like me to call you back, you know what to do."

This wasn't like him. When Morgan traveled for his business, she sometimes couldn't count on him answering the phone if it had slipped between the seats of his FJ60 Landcruiser or when he'd left it inside his gym bag. But on duty, like he was now, he kept his phone in his pocket at all times.

Not tonight. He must be distracted by something or *someone*.

She wouldn't think about that right now. Nor would she want to think about why, as soon as the words had left the doctor's mouth, she'd wanted to tell her mother.

How could she abandon me like this? And now

Morgan when I need him the most?

Annie dropped her weakened body down onto a kitchen chair and pressed her full lips together as her heart raced. All the blood drained from her round cheeks. Her mother had been at home when it had happened.

"It was her heart," the doctor had said. "She didn't suffer."

But it was all too sudden. Annie felt herself being pulled into a black hole.

Something wasn't right about this. And she was just supposed to take this man's word for it that her mother had died of a heart attack?

Annie caught her breath and dialed Morgan's number again one more time.

The room waited in relative silence. Chairs scraped the bay floors as men and a handful of women took their seats. Swallows from Pepsi bottles. Chuckling as expected from the back tables. A few cell phones buzzed. Not his. He'd left it on his bedside table that morning.

He cursed under his breath now, raking a strong hand over his dark brown, military style haircut then checked the Wenger on his wrist, his forearm muscles flexing beneath the polo uniform shirt he wore.

Putting this off wouldn't make it any easier.

That familiar ache of foreboding beat steadily through his chest. A grown man over six feet tall, who'd just completed CPAT, the Candidate Physical Abilities Test, in seven minutes, standing in a room full of his own kind shouldn't be this nervous. But he was. This he couldn't overcome with sheer physical strength.

They didn't judge him. They weren't there to grade him. This wasn't high school all over again.

But he couldn't stop the pounding of his heart. He couldn't breathe. He stepped up to the podium and cleared his throat.

Annie dragged herself up seventeen creaky steps and into her darkened bedroom. She'd barely reached the bed when the luminescent light from Morgan's side of the bed caught her eye. His phone display faced up.

She eyed the caller ID. "Who's Lara?"

She snatched it up to answer before whoever this woman was hung up. But the phone asked her to enter a passcode.

It stopped ringing. Moments later, a voice mail message chimed.

Annie picked up her own phone and dialed the fire department's number she had memorized long ago. Didn't her husband realize he'd left his phone at home?

"Is Morgan there?"

The deep, masculine voice on the other end of the line belonged to a stranger. "He's in training. Want me to tell him to call you back, Lara?"

Annie closed her eyes. Her entire world came to a screeching halt. Before she spoke she willed her heart rate to settle. "No, just tell him his phone's at home."

The man started to speak again before she hung up, but she didn't care. She didn't want to hear the reason he'd called her by that woman's name.

She marched out of her cottage, past the cluster of palm trees at her backyard, and down past the deep sand dunes where beach grass grew, its sharp spikes brushing past her calves. Into St. Michael's deep sand, still warm from the noon day sun, it was low tide and the beach was long. She reached the hard-packed sand where the water cooled the bottoms of her feet, so cool that a chill raced through her body, sending goosebumps skating across her skin. All the way down to the water she went, her purpose the same as it had been since her husband abandoned her, to let it lift her into its weightlessness, to let the salt wash away her scars, and to let it grip her naked body like an infant in the caress of its mother's bosom.

"A very famous physicist (just the mention of that word caused Morgan to sneer inwardly) tells us that there may be no such thing as an event horizon and therefore no black holes. Black holes, as they are thought of now, are inescapable chasms in space or at the very least a temporary detainment so destructive that whatever is sucked inside will become unrecognizable, like a book that has been burned in a house fire, sudden and inevitable death to all matter. Science has described the event horizon as the point at which a black hole becomes inescapable, its edge, the point of no return that surrounds it. In firefighting, we define the event horizon as the point at which the firefighter must turn back or face his or her death. The standard 2,226 psi airpack contains thirty minutes of air. If the firefighter pushes past the point of no return, the fire becomes inescapable, just like the event horizon, because they risk running out of air before they can get back out. How far can we as firefighters go before being sucked into a fire's black hole, never to return or spit out in far too mangled a state to be recognized? That's what every firefighter must be keenly aware of."

She hadn't been able to stand the solitude of her own house any longer, alone with her thoughts, the ticking of the clocks.

Annie preferred the night. No harsh light from the sun burned her scars. Florida's sun, merciless in the daytime, heated the sand to unbearable temperatures. Even the moon hid itself from the beach tonight. But the reflection in her mind's eye sparkled despite that. She could enjoy the beach without the heat. She could revel in the coolness of the wet sand in the dark.

Her neighbor's lights were out; they wouldn't see her remove her clothes. No one but she saw the white blouse with red English country rose pattern lying on the sand where she'd dropped it, the khaki skirt beside it covering beige silk panties and matching lace-trimmed bra.

Annie waded into the surf, letting the salt from the Gulf wash over her. The water, a thousand hands, simultaneously lifted her. She was never alone with the rushing tide, surrounded by the moving sand and tumbling waves.

She took a deep breath and dove. The salt and sound of her tears were swallowed up inside the wave. She pushed ahead, her arms breaking the current before her. Further and further she pushed, trying to see just how far and how long she could stay under this time without surfacing. Her heart pounded. Her chest ached. Her breath came in a gasp as she broke the surface of the water. A part of her mourned the fact that she had not gone farther. But tonight, it was not only her strength that had let her down, it was her husband.

"The new Scott SCBA is lighter and more ergonomic. It fits the contours of the firefighter's body. No more bumping into walls in the dark and knocking your mask off. And because of this design change, the need to be constantly aware of the event horizon becomes all the more pressing. These slimmer tanks can hold 4,500 pounds per square inch. That's almost twice the pressure than traditional airpacks, which hold 2,216 psi. Most fire scenes require a firefighter to enter, access, and exit all within two minutes. One hundred twenty seconds is a hell of a long time if you're playing hide and seek."

Chuckles stirred around the room, and Morgan took his first deep breath.

The bay doors of Eastview Fire Department's Station 2 were open now and the smell of the pork barbeque supper being set up at the back on several long folding tables overrode all of their attention spans.

"Safe return of every firefighter is of the upmost importance," Morgan continued, knowing his time was almost up. "That two minutes gives every firefighter on scene a road map. Because of our new RIT, rapid intervention team, downed firefighters have a fighting chance. Victims don't have the benefit of airpacks and we can't afford to lose a minute. But as much as we may want to, we can't just go charging in, as you are all well aware, and risk losing a firefighter. I'm not telling any of you anything you don't already know, but it's vital to stay constantly aware of why we do what we do. A hero sacrifices personal concerns for the greater good, not him or herself. That being said, the event horizon for the new airpacks is fifteen minutes, the maximum number of minutes, and again, the size of the firefighter using it and the level of excitement are both major factors. That's fifteen in and fifteen out. Further than that and you risk death. A maximum of thirty minutes. That's the same amount of air as the old ones just under higher pressure. But combined with our infrared cameras, the recon teams should be inside the structure removing victims well within five minutes. If we push too far, if we lose sight of the horizon, we risk damage that was after all avoidable. Physicists are uncertain if event horizons actually exist. But ask any firefighter, and they will tell you that they absolutely do."

Morgan removed the microphone clip from the lapel of his lieutenant's shirt and a cool trickle of sweat ran down the muscled valley of his back. He took another steadying breath.

It was over now.

Firefighters rose from their seats and headed to the back of the bay for their supper.

He wouldn't have to give another talk for a month.

A long time from now. Plenty of time to forget.

He looked at the Wenger on his wrist again. Seven o'clock.

What was she doing now?

An hour passed as if it were five minutes, breast-stroking the length of the beach, letting her body drift, allowing the water to consume her shock at losing her mother, and asking the Universe for a sign that she was not alone.

As she walked out of the waves, her naked body dripping with the healing salt water, a conch rolled out of a retreating wave and came to an abrupt stop at her foot. Even without light, she could see that the shell, old and worn out, gray and without life, was scratched and weathered like she was. Seven years ago, when she had been at her peak, newly graduated from college, her life ahead of her, that shell would also have been full of life, thriving. But today, both were hollow and empty.

Tempted to just carry her clothes the few yards back to her house, she rationalized that no one else would care either. No one would find her nudity alluring anymore. No longer was she the young woman she'd been when she'd met her husband. Even though the majority of St. Michaels was conservative, no one would take offense at seeing her naked breasts from their living room windows.

Why should they care anymore than I do?

"Good talk." Chief Wesley Gant's sixty-year-old hand slapped Morgan's powerful shoulder. "How's business?"

"Can't complain. If things continue on the way they have, I'll be able to add Tallahassee Fire and Rescue to my sales before the end of the month."

"Fine group of people down there." The older man steered him to the back of the bay towards the stacks of white buns, aluminum trays of shredded pork, coleslaw, and baked beans. "I know their chief. I can put in a good word for you."

"Thanks, chief. I'd appreciate that." Morgan watched the chief pile coleslaw on top of his pulled pork sandwich. "I haven't managed to get past their training officer yet."

"Don't think a thing of it. You're a good man and a good firefighter. We're lucky to have the best SCBA salesman in the southeast working for us here."

Taylor Armstrong, one of the newest hires, sauntered up to the table for a plate behind Morgan. "Lieutenant Morgan, your wife called during training."

Morgan's brow creased. "What'd she say?"

"That you left your phone at home."

Morgan cursed under his breath.

"How is Annie?" Eddie Stanton's creased cheeks and brown hair with a few grays stood out beside Taylor's cherub face and buzzed hair. "I haven't seen her in ages."

Taylor slapped his own forehead with the palm of his hand. "I thought your wife's name was Lara."

Morgan cursed audibly this time. "Why would you think that?"

"I'm sorry," Taylor said. "Every time that Lara woman calls here, I've thought she was your wife. I hope I didn't get you into any trouble at home because of this."

"Don't worry." Morgan blew out a breath. "I can handle it."

The time had come to clear the air with Annie anyway. Too many things had been left unsaid for too long. The opportunity he needed had just arrived.

Annie shoved her bra and panties into the pockets of her skirt and carried her brown leather sandals in her left hand. The breeze from the horizon dried her skin, but some of the sheer fabric of her blouse clung to water droplets here and there.

Renewed, at least for tonight, Annie showered alone in the master bathroom. Her wet hair wrapped in a towel and her terry cloth robe cinched around her waist, she placed her new treasure on the antique end table beside her bed, the last thing she saw before she switched off the gooseneck lamp.

In the dark, she listened to the waves outside. It had started to rain. Even over the sound of the ocean, she could hear the raindrops hitting the cottage's roof.

What is he doing now?

There had been a time when she would have known. He would have invited her down to the station for supper on a Sunday night. Seven years wasn't a long time to be married, but sometimes it was.

She pictured the old gray conch in her mind. A leap of faith. The way it had leaped from the waves. She must too.

But how?

Chapter 2

"So, there's not going to be a funeral?" Bryant Smith's dark-ringed blue eyes looked directly down into hers.

"No." Annie shook her head. "My mother didn't want one. Her body's going to be cremated this afternoon. I've canceled all my classes for the day. I don't even know what I'm doing here. I guess I just needed..."

A tear trailed down one of Annie's colorless cheeks.

"You look tired." Bryant lifted a hand, tracing a circle of eyelet on her shoulder. The fabric had barely given way before she recoiled.

His pale blue eyes sparked fire. "Is *he* allowed to touch you?"

"What kind of a question is that?" Annie's brow furrowed.

"An honest one from a man who's been used before." His eyes remained fixed on hers.

"Not by me."

"Making me the loser." He grinned, crossing his arms over his chest, the fabric of his dress shirt pulling tightly over his tan, sinewy forearms.

"Bryant, you mean the world to me. I'd be a mess right now if you weren't here. You know that."

"Then prove it." He took a step closer to her.

His cologne filled her nostrils and her gaze dropped to the floor. It had been a long time since any man had asked her to prove her feelings.

"Come with me."

Standing in his office doorway, she gazed past his eyes that watched her and around his right shoulder. The bare bones of the space jumped out at her now. Books missing from the shelves, personal effects gone, and where his laptop usually sat front and center on top of his desk, a brochure from the International Center for Theoretical Physics in Italy sat in its place. The changes should have tipped her off, but she'd been like a lost child since the phone call yesterday; she hadn't noticed until that moment.

"Without you with me, this trip will feel like nothing but work. I need my buddy to eat rigatoni with, to sight-see with. Don't make me go to the Colosseum alone. I'll feel like a tourist."

Annie sighed. "I can't go with you. I've got so many things to do my head is spinning."

Bryant interrupted her, gently tugging on the lapel of her blouse with his index finger and thumb.

He had sexy hands; she'd always thought so, long and tan.

"You can. It'll be good for you to get away from all your worries."

"I don't have a research grant. The university would never let me."

"No, but I have the university's permission to bestow my generosity upon the colleague of my choice."

Annie shook her head and looked down at the coffee-stained carpet beneath her ballet flats. Subtle brown waves of hair fell across her shoulders, brushing her cheeks. She sighed. "No, it would mean that I'd given up, and I haven't—not yet."

Bryant reached for her chin to make her look at him, but again she dodged. "It wouldn't mean that at all. Don't you at least deserve a break? Morgan gets breaks all the time while you're left at home."

Annie looked up into Bryant's light, almost gray, blue eyes. "That's true."

"Where is he right now?"

Annie took a deep breath, trying to remember what she'd written on her kitchen calendar. "Sarasota. I think." He'd come home long enough to pick up his phone that morning, she'd noticed. Conveniently while she'd still been asleep.

"See? He's on vacation. You're at work. Is that fair?"

"He's working. And besides, how would I explain a trip? Math teachers don't take research trips."

"No, but physicists do."

"Of which I am not."

"Look, Annie, it's not a question of how. It's why. Why not?"

Annie looked down again. In her mind she could see only the face of the young firefighter she'd married seven years ago. She shook her head, not at the memory, but at the man standing in front of her. "I just can't. That's why not."

Bryant heaved a sigh, his nostrils flaring. He stepped back into his office and reached for the doorknob. "I'll email you when I get there."

"I'd appreciate that." Annie smiled, but he didn't look at her.

"Whatever." Morgan closed the office door as

she still stood there.

She watched from the side panel window as he flung himself into his chair like a little boy denied a trip to Disneyworld. "I'm not any happier about it than you are."

She stood there with nowhere to go and no one to talk to, and she remembered the conch shell. Take a leap of faith, it said to her, just as it had leaped from the waves last night. She had to do the same. All of a sudden, her plan materialized in her mind. She marched right into her supervisor's office.

A red bandana for a headband held Annie's brown hair back away from her face as she carried in the last of the cardboard boxes she'd scrounged from the cafeteria. Her office had reeked of bananas by the time she'd finished packing up all of her things. The refurbished Landcruiser she drove, the one Morgan had rebuilt for her a year into their marriage, had been stuffed full. She'd parked it in the backyard close to the kitchen door so that she could unpack. Otherwise, she would've parked inside the garage. Morgan kept his business' inventory in his half, but the other half he insisted she use to park her truck. He'd said he didn't want her getting caught in a thunderstorm and having to run inside the house.

Dave Adams, her supervisor, had taken her resignation better than she expected. "As long as I'm here, you've always got a job at the University of West Florida, Annie," he had said to her.

She had trusted him. Office politics hadn't meant much to him. He had come from a time when, according to him, university positions had been awarded to those best at their jobs not best as schmoozing. "Hard work," he used to say in the break room loud enough for all to hear, "speaks louder than ass-kissing."

Now the spare room upstairs in her beach cottage smelled of bananas too as she unpacked the remnants of her office. Every item she removed from the former banana box, she traded for something already inside the room. Her brass lamp from her desk replaced the antique porcelain elephant lamp on the bedside table. Her laptop replaced the changing pad. Books on math theory and philosophy replaced rhyming board books. A stack of textbooks she'd taught from over the past seven years replaced an unopened warehouse-sized box of newborn diapers. Manila folders to fill an entire file cabinet replaced unopened packs of onesies. An old clock she'd found on an antiquing trip with Bryant replaced a gray elephant with a clock face in its side. And a photo of herself and Morgan on their wedding day replaced an empty picture frame awaiting the image of the baby they'd never conceived. Seven years had been a long time to try.

Now she had a pile of things she didn't know what to do with.

"In math, we call those things we don't know unknowns," she had said a thousand times to classrooms full of freshmen. She had given that lecture so many times, she'd memorized it. "Givens are the things we already know that can be applied to finding solutions to our problems."

Her unknowns were her husband. Where was he? And Lara. Who was she? The only given she had right now was a lonely house full of dashed hopes.

Dressed in the white tank top and khaki shorts she'd changed into after returning home, she crossed her arms over her chest as the ache returned. Every time she walked into this room, that longing came over her and wouldn't leave until she returned to the ocean to let the salt water wash it away. As she looked at Morgan wearing his tux in the wedding photo, the longing became exponentially more painful. On the verge of losing him, she didn't know how to make it stop.

"Since you don't want to try hormones, you need to get away from your usual routine," her doctor had said. "Lots of my patients have gotten pregnant on cruise ships, at hotels, or bed and breakfasts. You must take time off."

She chuckled aloud to herself now. "I'm taking plenty of time off now, doc."

"Since there's no medical diagnosis for your not conceiving," he had said, "it's likely to do with the post-traumatic stress of your attack all those years ago. So, you must take the necessary steps to alleviate your depression. I don't want to throw pills at you. In my day, we didn't have all these pills. If you were sad, you had a drink. If you were anxious, you had a drink."

"You sound like my mother. Her answer to everything is a glass of port."

He'd chuckled. "Have you tried it?"

"I don't drink."

"Well, you're probably better off. Your own mind has the power to overcome this with time."

Now she plugged in her laptop. "Depressed," she

said the word aloud, sounding it out. The screen lit up and she pulled the rocking chair over to it. The waist-high rectangular white dresser with painted knobs would have to serve as a desk until she could find a real one. Maybe she and Bryant could try that antique store downtown. No, Bryant was gone for the next year, a very long time to wait. Seeing him and talking to him every day since middle school when they'd met would be a hard habit to break. He'd been like the big brother she didn't have, apparently a reluctant one.

The laptop's screen said she had messages. Just as she'd hoped, an email from Bryant awaited her. "Thought you'd appreciate this bad physicist joke," the subject line read.

He must have already forgiven her for not going with him. Unlike the time back in college when she'd broken a dinner date with Bryant to go to the movies with UWF's quarterback. He'd avoided her and ignored her phone calls for weeks. Then suddenly, one Saturday morning as rain poured down outside, he'd knocked on her dorm room door, soaking wet, holding a box of Publix doughnuts in one hand and a handful of DVDs in the other.

She opened the email now and laughed aloud. Then below the cartoon image, she found the words, "I know you're going through a lot right now with losing your mother and whatever it is that Morgan is doing. An elephant never forgets. So remember, you're never alone, Annie. I'm just a message away."

An elephant never forgets. Her mother used to say that to her, and Bryant had always found it amusing.

Never alone, huh?

She looked around herself at the stacks of baby things she no longer needed, no longer wanted to look at because they reminded her of what she could not have.

"Then why am I alone?" she typed.

A stab of hunger shot through her as she closed her laptop. She looked at her watch, a smaller replica of the silver Wenger that Morgan wore. Well past noon, she meandered down the white wooden stairs to the kitchen.

They'd bought matching watches for each other as gifts for their wedding day. On Morgan's card, he'd written, "Every time I look at it, I'll be grateful for every minute of my life I get to spend with you." She'd never forgotten those words, especially at times when she found herself away from him.

After she finished her Publix vanilla yogurt, one of about a dozen she'd brought home from the stash in her mini-fridge in her office, she picked up a dust rag and a bottle of bergamot from her cleaning bucket. She headed back upstairs.

This would get rid of the banana smell and attract a new future. "I could use one."

Her laptop email had a new message light on it. "You say the word," Bryant had written, "and I'll come back today."

Annie slumped into the rocking chair. He'd asked her to go away with him; that's how far their friendship had gotten away from her. They'd been teenagers together. They'd seen each other through first boyfriends and girlfriends. He'd seen her through one particular boyfriend and she lots of his girlfriends. She couldn't keep track of how many he'd had, except for the three years he'd been married. They'd just always been able to pick up the phone, even at eight o'clock on a Friday night. There had never been a solitary spark between them, just an innocent attraction like two children holding hands, comfortable. But apparently, there had been real feelings on his part, the reason she couldn't go with him.

Bryant didn't even know she'd quit her job.

Why tell him?

She had a whole year to think about how to break the news to him. A whole year to start talking to herself without him around.

"Where are you?" she wrote. "I want to hear all about Italy when you get there." She closed the laptop.

Maybe she and Morgan should take a trip. They'd never had a honeymoon. She had the savings account she'd set aside. Now they wouldn't need that college fund after all. She wouldn't need a lot of things now. She looked down at the box of baby things.

Annie carried the dust rag downstairs. Deciding where they should go on their belated honeymoon, she shook off the dust out the back door. There next to the white picket fence sat a dog. She'd forgotten to close the latch on the gate when she'd finished unpacking the back of her truck and moved it inside the garage.

The old dog looked tired and had obviously been outside for a while. Dirt from last night's rain had matted down his or her hair, the grayish color of her conch. Old, forgotten things seemed to find her this week.

"Are you hungry?" she said.

The dog stood and wagged in reply.

"I'll be right back."

She went inside for a bowl of water and dug around in the cabinet for something suitable to feed a dog. She had some cheese crackers.

They would do.

Bowl in one hand and box of fish crackers under her arm, she went outside and filled the blue plastic bowl with the hose.

The dog seemed to have been without water for some time. And after the first bowl disappeared, she refilled it, and that one disappeared as well.

She held out her palm filled with fish crackers, and without a moment's hesitation, the dog took them. Annie spread a handful out on the deck and watched them quickly disappear too.

"Let's see who you belong to." Annie squatted down, reaching for the dog's collar.

He or she dipped his or her head and growled quietly but loud enough to get the point across.

"It's okay. I just want to see if there's an address or phone number." A round silver tag hung from the collar and read, Glenda.

"The good witch. Well, if that's you, you're welcome to stay the night. I could use all the help I can get."

Glenda licked her hand.

"I don't imagine you know where you belong, but that's okay. We'll put a notice in the paper and call the shelter and the police department. Someone is probably worried sick about you." Annie stood.

Long eyebrows moved with her. Sparkling, dark brown eyes looked up at her.

"Well, if you're staying the night, I'll make you a bed downstairs, but I must insist you bathe first."

Annie went back inside for a bar of Castile soap and one of Morgan's old beach towels. Under the hose, brown water ran from the poor thing's wiry coat, and Annie's hands were covered in brown bubbles as she scrubbed. When the water finally ran clear Annie could see patches on Glenda's elbows that were deeply calloused, and on her sides the blond hair had been worn away. Likely she'd been sleeping on cement. She also had a scratch on her left side that could have come from passing through a broken fence, but Annie couldn't be sure.

"I've got scars from my past too," Annie said.

As she swiped a hand down Glenda's side to dry her, she felt a tell-tale bulge.

"Oh, my, you're a mother dog, aren't you? Or soon to be. No wonder you're so hungry."

Not completely dry but not dripping wet, Glenda happily followed Annie inside the cottage, tail wagging. Annie made a bed for her out of a spare pillow from the linen closet and set it inside a large, low-sided basket she had filled with pine cones last Christmas. She set it in the corner of the kitchen next to the refrigerator because it would be warmer there and away from air conditioner vents. Last, she put down a new bowl of water.

"If you're going to stay, you need real food, not crackers."

Annie started a shopping list on the white board on her refrigerator and put dog food at the top. Below that, she wrote squeaky toys, two bowls, and a leash. Next, she called a veterinarian close by and made an appointment for Glenda, giving them a description of her in case the owner called looking for her.

By the time Annie hung up the phone, Glenda had fallen asleep on her side. Her tired legs stuck out of the side of the basket, and Annie added dog bed to the shopping list.

Annie crept quietly up the wooden stairs to her new office where she found two local websites that allowed visitors to post descriptions of found dogs. When she finished, her email icon showed one new message. She clicked on it, hoping Morgan had emailed her to explain why he'd snuck in that morning for his phone without a word to her. Of course, she had been sleeping at the time, but she still deserved an explanation, not that they'd given each other explanations in a long while.

"I miss hearing your sexy voice already," Bryant had written. "I'm in the airport. I'll call when my plane lands."

Annie didn't hit reply. She didn't know how to tell him that when he returned a year from now, they would no longer be work pals. She wouldn't be there to have lunch with him in her office every day or sit with him through endless professional development meetings.

She trudged down the stairs, trying to be as quiet as she could on the old creaky steps. Glenda needed her rest. That sounded familiar. Her doctor had said the same to her. She peeked into the kitchen from the living room and could see that Glenda had not moved and still slept peacefully. Annie sat down next to her on the floor. She couldn't resist stroking the dog's soft, beige head.

Annie had always wanted a dog, a friend to come home to, to talk to, someone to take walks with, and snuggle with at night. But she and her mother had lived in a duplex that didn't allow pets of any kind. And she had buried that want along with so many others that she'd forgotten about until now.

That ache in her chest returned. She couldn't wait until the sun went down so that she could go out to the beach and dive in, forgetting herself and her cares. If only the water could wash away her wounds the way the bath had washed the dirt from Glenda's body. There were scars on her own neck and hands that would never disappear. They were from another time and another place, one she would never return to, but a time and place in her memory that she could never forget because as a result she'd met her husband, her knight in shining armor.

She and her boyfriend had been broken up for about a month. He'd called her at her home a few times, but she'd refused to speak to him. Her mother would answer for her and try to explain to him that he needed to move on with his life. Finally, he'd threatened her mother, saying that if she didn't tell him where Annie was, he'd kill her. Obviously, the breakup had been harder on him, his life already a mess from his new habit of drinking excessively. He'd seen other women at parties behind her back, but she'd been too naïve and inexperienced to notice. Eventually he dropped out of college to smoke weed full-time. Annie couldn't drop him fast enough.

"I could've told you that," Bryant had said when

she'd told him her reasons for breaking off the relationship. "He was a loser, Annie. You could do a lot better than him."

The summer Annie had met Morgan she'd been a mermaid. The Deep Sea Dive, a dock-side restaurant on the Gulf, had hired her to swim in a wall-sized tank to entertain guests while they ate.

Morgan had been a young firefighter of twenty-six at the time. At three o'clock that afternoon when she had started her shift, the fire department truck had arrived for a routine inspection of the exits, fire extinguishers, and wiring. That's when she'd first seen Morgan. From inside the tank, she'd caught him staring. She wore a shell bikini top and fins, actually a green body suit that covered her from her waist to her feet. And a lot of men had stared at her that summer. When she'd surfaced, three firemen had been in the back speaking to her boss, Wade Biggins, a stocky, middle-aged man with a jowly face and crew cut. The Marine Corps tattoo on his shoulder showed beneath the short-sleeved dress shirts he wore. Morgan had been among the firemen speaking to Wade in the store room.

She'd gotten out of the tank and put on a robe not from shyness but because Wade kept the temperature sixty-eight degrees back there. Morgan had held a clipboard and asked her a few questions about the tank.

Still in college, she'd been hired for the summer. But if she liked it, she'd stay on through the fall semester. The money was good. And although her mother wouldn't let Annie pay her own way through college, Annie had insisted on having a job after watching her mother cut back on expenses while driving her fifteen-year-old Subaru.

Annie had answered Morgan's questions and been impressed by his manners. Although she had been wearing fins and shells when he'd first seen her, he'd looked her in the eyes as she spoke and continued to as he asked his questions despite the fact that her robe clung to her, soaked along with the rest of her body. He could have seen straight through the flimsy white robe, but he didn't. He'd only looked at her face and spoke to her with respect, something she'd never gotten from her ex.

She'd watched Morgan leave the restaurant that day and get into the huge red fire engine with the number 2 printed in yellow letters on its doors. And after spending the rest of the afternoon thinking about Morgan, she'd even called Bryant on her break to tell him that she'd met someone.

"Don't tell me you're going to marry a fireman and have two kids and a white picket fence. I'll lose my lunch." Bryant had never been one to want to settle down, still hadn't.

At eleven o'clock that evening, the restaurant closed. She went out to her car in the parking lot alone as she always did, only this time singing the words to *Take My Breath Away*. It had rained all afternoon and the parking lot's pavement glistened in the light from the back door, but she didn't even notice the puddles as she splashed through them in her slip-on sandals.

She hadn't seen her ex waiting in the darkness to jump out at her from behind her car, a hunting knife in his hand. She'd screamed and slipped on the wet asphalt, falling backwards and losing one of her sandals in the process.

"Shut up! I just want to talk to you," he'd said, the smell of liquor from his breath filling her nostrils. "You won't take my calls. I didn't have a choice. You have to give me another chance."

Lifting herself up on her knees, she backed away from him and reached for her car door, shaking fingers fumbling with the key.

"Please, Annie." All the air left her lungs as he jumped her.

She'd screamed again, this time the hunting knife's black jagged blade pressing against the delicate skin of her throat. He yelled at her to shut up, but it had done no good. The harder he pressed, the harder she screamed. She couldn't stop. The knife's cool blade sliced into her neck, making smooth cuts like ice on her skin in the damp humidity.

When Wade finally heard her screams and opened the back door, he found Annie pinned to the asphalt, fighting for her life. Wade shouted to one of his cooks to call 911 and charged out the door towards her.

The police were tied up in another area, but when the dispatcher discovered there were injuries involved, she sent the fire department.

Wade had tackled her ex, taking him down with a head and shoulder to his abdomen. Both men had landed feet away from her on the blacktop.

Blood trickled from her fingers. The knife had sliced into her palms, wrists, and arms, everywhere she looked hadn't escaped his wrath.

When she'd opened her eyes inside the

ambulance, Morgan's smiling face had hovered above her. He spoke to her in his deep voice, whispered to her that she would be okay, all the while, tearing open endless packages of cotton bandages. He caressed her cheek with the backs of his fingers whenever she closed her eyes and told her she would be alright. When they arrived at the hospital, he walked inside beside the gurney, not leaving her side until the ER nurses took over.

But Morgan hadn't stopped there. The next morning, he was back. The next afternoon, he came again. He visited her in the hospital every day for two weeks. He asked her to have dinner with him as soon as she got out of the hospital. She'd said yes.

Now the sound of the cottage's front door opening and closing brought her out of her memory. Every time she thought of her ex, she wished him well in state prison.

From the kitchen Annie heard the sound of Morgan's footsteps filling the small cottage.

So he'd finally come back home.

Her hero.

Chapter 3

Annie still sat next to Glenda on the kitchen's tile floor. No dinner had been made; she hadn't expected Morgan home. She never expected him home any more. A text here and there let her know occasionally that he still lived and breathed. The fire department and hotel rooms had become his home three years ago when he'd started his business, the same time they'd realized that trying to have a baby wasn't working.

He searched for her; she could tell by the route his footsteps made through the house, first the living room, then the office. When they neared the kitchen, the muscles in the back of Annie's neck tightened. Whatever he had to say to her must be important.

"What's this?" Morgan's voice sounded strained.

"And by that I assume you mean *who* is this?" Annie said.

He nodded curtly.

"This is Glenda. She's going to be staying with us, with me, for a little while. She's lost and tired and pregnant." She'd meant for her tone to sound final, not asking if he had any objections to the newcomer, but telling him.

Morgan turned from the kitchen, likely heading for the shower.

"Who's Lara?"

Her words stopped him, froze him in place. His broad shoulders remained stiff as ever, refusing to give her any satisfaction. She'd hit a nerve though.

He still hadn't spoken, his back to her. He would explain Lara to her, though Annie doubted very much she wanted to hear the explanation. But as his silence stretched, he confirmed her fears.

Finally, he heaved a deep breath and turned. There were dark circles under his blue eyes that weren't usually there. His skin, tan from working out of doors, could not conceal them. But she stuck to her resolve.

"She's an employee of one of the companies we do business with."

"You mean *you* do business with."

Again he nodded curtly. The muscles in his neck and shoulders and forearms were tight.

Good, let him feel as horrible as I do.

"Taylor made a mistake, that's all. He thought you were a business call."

Annie crossed her arms over her chest. "Is that right? Why would he assume it was her and not me?"

"Because you never call the station."

"And this Lara person does?"

"Sometimes."

"Has she been to the station?"

Morgan obviously had not been expecting that. He drew back.

"Just how much is going on between the two of you?" Annie's voice sounded hollow.

"There's nothing going on between the two of us. There is no us."

"I don't want to be lied to. I want the truth, Morgan. Why do you keep a password lock on your phone?"

"I'm on the road a lot, Annie. If I lose my phone,

I don't want someone accessing our bank account."

"You also don't want your wife seeing your texts."

"What kind of a thing is that to say to me? I haven't done anything wrong."

"Neither have I. That's why I don't keep my phone locked."

"You should. You work around a lot of young people who know what to do with that kind of information."

"They're not hackers, Morgan. And I don't work around them anymore."

"What do you mean?"

"I quit my job this morning."

"What? Why didn't you tell me about this until now?"

Because my mother died, my husband is currently cheating on me, and my relationship with my best friend reached the breaking point.

She uncrossed her arms and got up from the floor. "That's a good question. And I've got one for you. Why did you sneak into the house this morning for your phone?"

"You were sleeping. I didn't want to wake you."

Annie scoffed. "I didn't tell you because you were working. I didn't want to bother you with trivialities from my life. Not that you asked, but the reason I called, when Taylor mistook me for your mistress, was because my mother died last night." Her voice rose high over her choking, beating heart. "She had a heart attack." The last few words came out on a broken sob.

Morgan rushed to her, scooping her up from the

cold, hard tile floor into his arms. "Why didn't you tell me?" he whispered into her hair, holding her tightly. "I would've come right home."

"She had a strong heart. She wouldn't have had a heart attack. There's something wrong."

"What do you mean, Annie? Wrong with what?"

"With what the doctor said. She didn't die of a heart attack. I know she didn't. That's too easy."

"If I remember correctly, your mother's diet left a lot to be desired."

The stairs groaned beneath the combined weight of Annie's slight frame and Morgan's much larger one.

"No, Morgan." Her voice was pleading as she clung to him. "She was healthy. She'd just had a checkup. There wasn't a thing wrong with her." She couldn't speak anymore through the onslaught of tears, because as much as she wanted to believe that his rationale was correct, her doubts were much too loud to let her.

Within minutes, Morgan had Annie tucked into a bath with a cup of chamomile tea on the side of the tub while he went downstairs to make dinner. Being a fireman all these years had made him a good cook. In just a few minutes, he had two egg and mushroom omelets with onion and red bell peppers made. He sprinkled a little shredded cheddar over both and carried them upstairs on a tray.

Annie stood in the bathroom doorway wrapped in a terry cloth robe, looking lost.

"Into bed with you."

Annie did as he ordered, tucking her feet in and

sitting up against the pillows.

Morgan set the tray in front of her with their omelets, whole wheat toast, her favorite butter spread, and apricot jam. Morgan ate his omelet with dry toast and a glass of water while Annie indulged herself. All the crying she'd done left her with a deep hole inside that needed filling. And right now, butter and jam would do.

When their plates were empty, Annie watched Morgan dust his hands of toast crumbs and the hollowness returned. Did Lara sit this close to him in bed? Did they share breakfasts, lunches, and dinners together too?

At least seventy percent of Morgan's life she never saw. What hotel did he prefer? Did he use the hotel weight rooms for his workouts? Who did he talk to late at night?

"How did you meet her?"

Morgan looked at Annie with raised brows. "Who?"

"You know who."

"Let's not talk about that right now. You need to rest."

"I'm not tired."

"You just don't feel it yet because you're in shock."

Annie crossed her arms. "I've been in shock before." Even in and out of consciousness, she'd heard the paramedic in the ambulance say that she was in shock. "This doesn't feel the same."

She'd known that one day she would lose her mother. Even as a girl, she'd tried to prepare herself for the inevitability. "When are you going to die?"

she'd asked her mother.

"I try not to think about such things, dear." She'd laughed. Then without another word she'd continued combing out the hair of the older woman sitting in the barber's chair.

The answer had been Earth-shatteringly important to little Annie, and her mother had shrugged off her question as if it had been a gnat.

"It's best to take it easy anyway," Morgan said now, leaning back beside her on the pillows, brushing her arm as he moved.

She scooted away from him and a cloud passed over his blue eyes, turning them as dark as the ocean before a storm.

"Why'd you want quit your job?"

Annie couldn't tell him the real reason, that Bryant had asked her to go to Italy with him, because that would lead to questions like, did she want to go? Nothing but friendship had ever been between them. But she had come to depend on Bryant when her nights at home alone had become too frequent. Did that mean she loved him?

"It's time to move on, that's why," she said. "I've got my savings. So we don't have to worry about that."

"I'm not worried. I'm just sorry you couldn't talk to me about it first." Morgan put his hands behind his head against the wrought iron bed frame and let his head fall back as he stared up at the painted wooden beams in the cathedral ceiling, the muscles in his biceps rippling with the motion.

Morgan never seemed to worry about anything. Maybe that was his trouble, he should be worried about their marriage.

"Why didn't you say anything about this to me before?" he said.

"Why didn't you tell me about Lara?"

Morgan blew out a long breath. "There's nothing to tell."

"Then tell me everything there isn't to tell."

Morgan closed his eyes, not ignoring her, but preparing himself. "She's in charge of buying for Gray Scales. They're a large industrial company. The reason she called the station was to get some figures that I had promised her but forgot."

"How'd she get the station's number? I thought you did business with your cell."

"I do. I guess she looked it up in the phone book."

"Why didn't she call your cell phone?"

"I don't know. Probably she did, but I didn't answer because I'd left it here."

She had seen Lara's name appear on his phone's screen before she'd been blocked from answering it; he'd told her the truth about that. But her heart still ached.

His phone rang in his pocket now.

Annie held her breath as he looked at the screen.

"It's my mother."

Annie crossed her arms over her chest.

"I've got to answer it," he said. "She called while you were in the shower. She asked me to ask you if she should come down."

"No thanks. I can find enough things wrong with me without her help."

Morgan sighed. He spoke into his phone with his

deep, resounding voice.

Since Annie had grown up without a man around the house, when she'd first married him, she would sit on the sofa, listening to his voice from the kitchen as he spoke on the phone to his mother, his sister, whoever, just as long as he kept talking. All the nights they'd fallen asleep in bed talking about anything, nothing, those times were gone. So she hung on his every word now.

When he hung up, his phone rang again. This time when he looked at the screen he said nothing.

"It's her again, isn't it? Aren't you going to answer it?"

"I don't need to. I know why she's calling."

"Well, I don't."

"It's business, Annie."

"Then answer it."

His nostrils flared as he blew out a breath. The ringing stopped. "It went to voice mail."

"Convenient."

"What the hell does that mean?"

"You didn't want to answer it in front of me."

"So what if I didn't? You should know how that feels. Your *pal*, Bryant, is never too far out of reach."

Bryant had been there that fateful night to see Annie at the restaurant. He had left long before her shift had ended; he'd had a date with yet another woman that night. But much later, he'd called Annie's cell phone, probably to tell her how badly the date had gone. Morgan had answered it in the ambulance. She'd forgotten that until now. Then Bryant had come to see her at the hospital.

"But I don't hide anything from you," Annie said

now. "That's the difference. You know who Bryant is; you've met him. He was at our wedding. How long have you known her?"

"I've tried to tell you; I don't *know* her."

"Well then when did you meet her?"

"Long after you met Bryant," he said with staid calmness.

"I see. Does this mean you're jealous of Bryant?"

"No."

"Okay, then why..."

"Look, Annie," he said, interrupting, "I'll tell you because I know you're not going to let this go until we account for every second of every day I've spent since I met Lara."

Annie closed her mouth.

"Her boss bought the three of us dinner the first night I was in town."

"What town?"

"Gulf Breeze. That was three months ago."

"December. That was the night we celebrated when you came home."

The last time they'd made love. Morgan had come home with a bottle of wine. He'd been so happy.

Morgan nodded. "We were celebrating that sale. They're a huge supply chain for fire departments all over the Southeast. Business has been more than good since I landed this account. So, that's how it started. She's in charge of purchasing. She has my number for questions her boss asks, for anything the company needs."

"I see. And have you seen her since that night."

Morgan let out an audible breath. "Yes."

"How many times?"

"A few."

"How many is a few?"

"Three, I guess. Okay?"

"And in what context?"

"What context?" Morgan's brow creased and his face had taken on a darker shade of red.

"What were the two of you doing the times you saw each other?"

"Having dinner."

Annie's stomach dropped. She looked at his left hand. He'd never made a habit out of wearing the gold band they'd bought before their wedding. Wearing a ring represented a hazard in his line of work. Too many things for it to get hung up on.

"Does she know you're married?"

"She does now."

"What do you mean?"

"It means that I told her."

"When?"

"Last night."

Annie closed her mouth before a tirade of questions spilled out about why he'd phoned Lara and not his own wife. At least she knew now where she stood, second in line behind Lara.

"Why now? Why not before?"

"Because she asked."

"That's a pretty personal question for her to ask from a strictly business relationship, isn't it?"

"What do you want me to say?"

"Is she pregnant?"

"What the hell?" he said in a harsh, raw voice.

"Is she having your baby?"

Morgan's eyes opened wide as he stared at her, his breath puffed a strand of hair into her eyes.

Annie looked at him, the wild accusation between them now, no taking it back. It hadn't been a question she'd planned to ask. It had just all of a sudden come out. After trying for seven years to conceive, her mind had taken her there, the nightmare of Morgan having a tall, strong baby boy with another woman. Annie hadn't given him any children, maybe another woman had. It had seemed perfectly reasonable until she said it aloud.

"I can't believe you just said that to me." Morgan stood.

"Where are you going?"

"I came home to talk to you about what happened last night. I wanted to say that I'm sorry about the misunderstanding. But instead of coming home to my wife and having a heart-to-heart, I find out that you've quit your job, your mother is dead, and I'm the last to know. By the way, when did you tell Bryant?"

"Last night."

"Perfect." Morgan punched the bathroom's doorframe.

"That's only because he was home, and he answers his phone when I call."

"Yeah, he's a real dependable guy. The man's had more girlfriends than I can count. He's too old to still be acting like a kid."

"He just hasn't found the right woman yet."

"Oh, yes he has. He's found her. She's just married to someone else," he poked a finger at his chest, "me. And he got to her before I did."

Annie's mouth was still open as Morgan stormed

out of the bedroom.

He'd never admitted to being jealous before. Some of her anger slipped away. Had Bryant been a silent threat to him all these years?

The Landcruiser's engine sprang to life in the driveway. A part of her ran after him to ask him not to leave, but the other part of her stayed put because she didn't want to know where he was going. She looked down at the wedding band quilt with the yellowed background and red country roses that covered her legs. She tossed it aside and padded across the bare wood floor to the balcony. From the edge, she could look down at the street. Morgan's truck rolled to a stop at the corner and turned towards the center of St. Michaels.

She slumped into one of the rocking chairs where she and Morgan had watched the sun set over the ocean a thousand times. She looked down at the knee wall where the leg of her rocking chair had scratched the paint away one night. In a mad love-making frenzy, Morgan had shoved her chair out of their way and it had hit the wall. Every time she looked at that scratch, their naked bodies entwined popped into her mind. And every time she walked into the garage to pick up a paint brush to paint over it, she changed her mind. It wouldn't be right to gloss over a piece of their history. She wouldn't let go of anything else that was hers, especially her marriage.

This Lara woman, if she wanted Morgan, would have a fight on her hands. If she assumed she could waltz into their lives and steal her husband away, she was in for a rude awakening.

The quiet of the house closed in around her now.

Annie cinched the belt on her robe and picked her way to her new office.

If I were to die suddenly of a heart attack, the way the doctor claimed my mother had, who would notice?

She shoved that morbid thought away.

She and Morgan needed to reconnect, if for no other reason than to discover if they still had something worth holding onto. And now she'd made up her mind; they would have that honeymoon they'd never taken. She wasn't letting go yet.

Chapter 4

The next afternoon, Annie and Glenda left the vet's office, Glenda looking happily out of the Landcruiser's passenger side window as they turned onto 2400 Horizon Drive.

"This is going to be your new home now, for at least as long as you want to stay," she said as she pulled onto the shell-covered drive.

Inside the house, Glenda slowly made her way with her ever-expanding belly to her new bed. She and Annie had made the much-needed trip to the pet store that morning and purchased everything Glenda would need for her stay; however long it would be.

Glenda looked ready for a nap. So Annie replaced her bowl with fresh water and topped off her food. "Sleep, Glenda. You've earned it. You were a good girl at the vet's."

Annie sat down at the kitchen table as Glenda's dark brown eyes smiled up at her then closed in agreement. The dog took a deep breath and went to sleep.

With no more Friday afternoon movies, Saturdays on Bryant's boat, and Sundays antiquing to keep her mind off of her failing marriage, life would never be the same for Annie. Glenda's presence in her life suddenly took on a profound meaning. It meant that the piece of Annie's heart, the part that had been broken by her mother's death, could possibly reform.

Watching Glenda sleep in the corner next to the

refrigerator, the weight of responsibility for another living being crept in on her. She would do as much for the dog as she possibly could, but she didn't know if that would be enough. She'd never been domestic. Taking care of another living being seemed daunting.

Looking around her kitchen, she saw what wasn't there. She'd never learned to cook, something she wasn't proud of. She opened the pantry door, full of boxes of dried pasta and soup cans in disarray, stuffed in at odd angles and in some places, nearly falling off the narrow shelves. In the spare closet, a wedding gift from her mother sat unopened, a set of clear acrylic canisters with white lids no doubt from the QVC. The picture on the box showed dried beans in one and flour in another.

She could do that; she had those.

Behind the box slid out a card, one she'd obviously forgotten to open. She turned it over. In her mother's hand were written the words, *to be opened by Annie and Morgan on their seventh wedding anniversary.*

She remembered now her mother had given this to them on their wedding day. How had she forgotten?

Their anniversary was two months away. She put her index finger underneath the flap then stopped. It said to be opened by Annie *and* Morgan.

Morgan wasn't there and since he hadn't come home last night, she had to face reality—he might not come home.

She stuffed the morbid reminder that her mother was dead inside the kitchen drawer, unable to look at it any longer. She couldn't think about her right now, not while Morgan was away, not while her emotions were still so raw.

For now, to take her mind off of her mother, as she carried on with her plan for home improvement, she placed the box of containers on the kitchen table. As she pried it open with her fingers, she forced herself to repeat a little tune she'd heard Morgan humming last night from the bedroom as he'd prepared their dinner before storming out. Inside the box were twenty-four canisters of varying sizes. And emptying out the mismatched boxes of dry goods from the pantry into the canisters, with their clean lines, felt satisfying, like a new pair of shoes. When she'd finished, her pantry looked like a before and after picture in a Better Homes and Gardens magazine.

With that done, feeling somewhat better, Annie prepared for more domestic tasks to keep her mind occupied. She began a mental list of things she'd accomplish, like a cooking class. She could make dinner for herself and Morgan, instead of relying on cans of soup. Then she'd take a baking class since she would make Morgan's next birthday cake for him without her mother to make it.

She pulled out the canister of flour and raisins. She suddenly had a taste for muffins for her breakfast in the morning. Twenty minutes later, with her task complete and her counters covered in batter, Annie had a renewed sense of herself. She set the oven timer for twenty-five minutes, wiped the counters clean, and loaded the used bowls and spoons into the dishwasher. With nothing left to do but wait, she snuck up the creaky stairs so she wouldn't wake

Glenda, who'd slept through it all.

"Her puppies are due any day now," Annie typed.

She'd gotten the email from Bryant that he had safely arrived in Italy. She decided to instant message him today. "The vet said it wasn't her first litter and that she's pretty old to be having puppies. Maybe someone will say that about me one day. It's called a geriatric pregnancy. The ultrasound showed five puppies. So she offered to keep her there at the office until they're born. But I couldn't leave Glenda there. She came to my house, our house, for a reason. I know it." Annie attached a picture of Glenda before she hit send.

Bryant's reply took only a few seconds to arrive. "She's cute. And I know she picked the right person to move in with. It feels so good to hear from you, Annie. It was weird not seeing your smiling face this morning. And I have to wait a year to look into your beautiful blue eyes again."

Maybe even longer than that.

"How's the pasta?" she wrote.

"Better than you can imagine. And don't get me started on the gelato I had for dessert last night. I'm coming back to Florida with a paunch."

Annie laughed. "You? Never."

"How are you holding up?"

Annie sighed. "I don't know really. I don't know how I'm supposed to feel."

"Sounds like you're still in shock."

"You sound just like Morgan."

"How are things between the two of you?"

"Strained as usual."

"Tell me all about it."

"What can I tell you that you don't already know? Well, there's a woman. Lara. She's a business associate."

"Uh, huh. And since you know about her, I assume there's trouble there."

"I don't know how much of it I'm borrowing or if I really should be worried."

"Time will tell."

"I don't think I want to wait. I'm really upset about this. Before it was just his work that kept him away from me. I understood that. But now... it feels like more than that. Bryant, I don't want to end up all alone."

"What did I tell you about that? You're never alone. I'm here for you."

"I know. You're terrific. But... you know."

"It's not the same?"

"Exactly."

"Well, let me tell you this, if Morgan doesn't realize what he's got and soon, someone may just steal you away from his burly ass."

Annie laughed.

Bryant and Morgan had always been opposites in that way. Bryant had a svelte, understated sexiness that couldn't be truly appreciated until he took his t-shirt off while sailing his catamaran. But Morgan on the other hand, couldn't hide his attributes. They bulged from beneath his clothes, making him appealing from across the room. Sexuality emanated from both men.

Annie heard the timer going off in the kitchen downstairs.

"Gotta go," she typed in a hurry. "Email me tomorrow."

She rushed downstairs. Glenda still lay in the kitchen on her bed, but now on her side, whimpering.

"Uh, oh, Glenda, are you going to have your puppies today?"

Glenda didn't move, just moaned.

"The vet said any day. I guess that means today."

Glenda whimpered again.

Annie removed the very flat, very browned muffins from the oven and set them on the cooling rack. Then she went to the refrigerator.

"The vet gave me this medicine to give you when you went into labor. I'm not sure what it'll do for you, but it's worth a try." Annie lifted the edge of Glenda's cheek in a very undignified way, the way she'd been shown to do it. Just as the vet had demonstrated, she squeezed the contents of the syringe into the dog's mouth. Glenda compliantly swallowed the pink liquid and lay her head back down.

Annie sat down next to Glenda without crowding her. "I'm right here if you need me."

Glenda closed her eyes, resting between whimpers, which Annie took to be contractions. She at least remembered that much about childbirth from all the books she'd read.

Annie checked her cell to be sure the vet's number showed up on speed dial. Then putting her phone back in the pocket of her khaki shorts, she rested her head against the wall behind her. "Is this what it's like becoming a mother, lots of waiting?" She took a deep breath and settled in for a long day, for the both of them.

Hours had passed when Annie opened her eyes and looked at the clock. Her head rested along the edge of Glenda's bed and her shoulder ached like it never had. She'd never slept on the kitchen floor before.

Glenda continued to rest with her eyes closed.

Annie's stomach growled. She didn't want to wake Glenda. The sun had started to set, well past dinner time. She opened the fridge and pulled out a cherry vanilla yogurt. Very carefully, she pulled the utensil drawer open. As her hands closed over a stainless steel handle, Glenda yelped. Annie froze. Dropping the spoon, she rushed to Glenda's side. The vet had warned her not to get too close after signs of labor began.

"Dogs instinctively know what to do. But if you see signs of distress, call the office immediately."

What are distress signs?

Glenda didn't move and Annie pulled her phone from her pocket. Her finger hovered over the send button. Glenda finally moved. A spot of blood stained the light blue bed.

Annie ran to the linen closet and pulled out some old brown towels that had been Morgan's before they had moved in together. She'd never liked them.

On the towel appeared a blood-covered pup about the size of her hand. Annie scooted on the floor hesitantly towards her for a better look. The puppy's eyes were closed and so round and transparent she could almost see through the lids.

"Your baby!" Annie whispered over the lump in her throat as Glenda began licking the precious new arrival.

And not a moment later, another little pup appeared, and Glenda cleaned that one too. Another and another puppy arrived until finally, Glenda shared her new bed with her five perfect puppies.

Annie tucked the second old towel around Glenda's babies to keep the air conditioning from their little bodies.

Glenda looked grateful and especially worn out.

Annie sat back down next to Glenda's bed, a lightness around her heart she'd never known. "You're already a great mother, Glenda. Your babies are so lucky."

Annie's mother had always wanted to be a grandmother, though she'd never come right out and said it. She never missed a chance to tell Annie all about her friends' grandchildren who'd come to visit the hair salon. She heard her mother right there with her, saying now, "How precious!", the same thing she'd always said over new babies.

Annie turned off the kitchen light over the sink for Glenda's sake. She needed her rest now. The puppies were all sleeping peacefully at her side. Annie let the new mother and her pups sleep as she tiptoed into the living room and curled up on the couch and went to sleep herself.

In the morning, after pulling herself off of the couch with a crick in her neck, Annie looked in on the nursing puppies, showered, then changed into fresh clothes. As she dried her hair, she called Morgan, who still hadn't come home. His phone rang and rang until it went to voice mail. She hung up and texted him. After several minutes, she still had no reply.

Why doesn't Morgan answer his phone? Is he with Lara?

Annie's stomach growled, reminding her of the muffins she'd made yesterday. In the kitchen, she found them still resting on the cooling rack where she'd forgotten them. She poked one with her index finger. It didn't give an inch, as hard as a rock. She dumped the contents of the muffin tray into the trash can.

I've still had a lot to learn about domestic life.

Her Landcruiser's engine thrummed deep as she backed onto Horizon Drive. The truck had been a gift from Morgan on their first anniversary. Her little red Honda she'd had since college still ran well, but the air conditioner leaked freezing cold water onto the floorboards every time she went around a turn. Morgan said he could fix it for her. Then he'd surprised her by giving her the truck he'd worked so hard on. He'd spent every spare hour he had at the fire station (before his new business). Then one day he'd called her out to the garage, handed her the keys, and asked, "Ready to take your new truck for a test-drive?"

Now, she headed down Ocean Boulevard, the street running the length of St. Michaels, bordering the shore. Her cell phone rang at the next red light. She could see the name, Periwinkle Funeral Home, on the display, but she didn't have the stomach to answer. Once voice mail had retrieved the message, she parked her truck in front of Morgan's station, Eastview Fire Department, and played it.

"Your mother's remains are ready for you to pick up at your earliest convenience."

She cringed and pressed disconnect. She'd known this was coming, but she wasn't prepared.

Opening the front door to the station, the smell of coffee and frying oil met her, a smell that reminded her of happy times with Morgan, laughing and lingering over meals together. A few of the firefighters sat in the day room watching television or napping, likely due to a midnight call to a wreck or a carbon monoxide detector whose batteries had died in the wee hours of the night. When she peered her head inside, Eddie Stanton stood up first from his recliner.

"How you doing there, lady?" he drawled. "I was just telling Morgan we haven't seen you down here in too long." The lanky firefighter hugged her tight. She looked up into his handsome face about a foot above her and smiled. One of Morgan's oldest friends, they'd seen each other through a lot of dicey situations over the years.

"I'm looking for Morgan. He's having phone trouble."

A look that could have been pity passed over Eddie's face and he squeezed her shoulders before releasing her. "He was here. Left about a half hour ago. Said he was going to West Pines' Headquarters to talk to the chief there."

"Thanks, Eddie." She swung her purse over her shoulder.

"Tell Morgan he still owes me a Landcruiser."

Annie laughed. "Tell Tammy I said hi."

"Will do." He hugged her once more, this time lingering a moment longer. "Hey, take care of yourself." His voice held a soothing tone, as if he knew something she didn't. But she did.

Annie smiled up at the man who always remembered to wish her husband a happy birthday, the man who'd been there the day she met Morgan, the man who'd risked his life for her husband too many times to count.

As Annie drove out of St. Michaels towards West Pines Fire Department, she prepared what she would say to Morgan when she found him. She'd never followed him like this before, but she'd never been so desperate before. So far, none of their problems had gone away by ignoring them. And she didn't expect this one to either.

The roofline of the fire station came into view among the pine trees that surrounded it. Annie expected to have to explain herself when Morgan saw her there. What she hadn't expected was seeing Morgan's tall frame there in the parking lot of the station standing in front of a blond-haired woman. They were talking, standing too close. She was almost as tall as Morgan and wore a figure-hugging, fire engine red business suit. Lara. That had to be her.

Annie's heart tripled its rhythm. She looked down at the khaki shorts and pink rayon tank top she wore. Was that blood on her shorts?

The voice in Annie's head told her just to keep driving, to pretend she'd never been there and pass right by the two of them (they hadn't noticed her anyway). She should drive behind the station along the horseshoe drive, that encircled the back of the building, and go home. But she didn't.

Her hands shook as she turned the wheel, parking slowly. Everything around her seemed surreal. The pine trees, the sand beneath them, the boxwoods all stood out with startling clarity. She turned the key in the ignition, shutting off her truck's engine.

Morgan had seen her now, had heard her truck. He kept looking back in her direction, while obviously still talking to this woman, his attention torn between the two. Several times, she caught that woman trying to hide the fact that she stared.

Morgan met her at the front of her truck, leaving his Lara standing where she'd been. Annie's knees threatened to buckle out from beneath her as her feet touched ground. Curious firefighters inside the station had come to the windows and peered through the vertical slats in the blinds without touching them. Morgan noticed too.

"What are you doing here?" Morgan stood with legs planted wide apart, lips flattened into a thin line, and nostrils flared.

"I'm happy to see you too."

"Don't give me that." The ferocity of his tone frightened her as much as thrilled her. His eyes searched hers wildly. "Why are you here? Is something wrong?"

"What else could be wrong? I try to call you, you don't answer. I come looking for you, I find you with her." Annie gestured towards Lara, and as she did, caught the hint of a pleased smile on other woman's lips.

"I still don't know why you're out looking for me."

"You're my husband. I shouldn't have to look for you. I should be privy to your whereabouts. But it looks like for some reason, I'm the last to know. How did *she* find you?"

"Annie, you're upset. Go home. We can talk about this when I get there."

"Does that mean you're going to grace me with your presence at home?"

"What does that mean?"

"It means you're never there." Her voice rose and her whole body shook as her mind raced on. "And I can see now why, because you're with her."

"Are you trying to tell me that there haven't been times, too numerous for me to count, that you and Bryant haven't been off gallivanting around together? Times when I came home from work not knowing where you were, only that you were with him? An offhand note, written by him no less, on the fridge. And me with no way to find you."

"There's one big difference, Morgan. I've never once," she held up her index finger, "not once done anything behind your back. And I never wanted to."

Morgan released a breath. "Look, this isn't the time or the place for this. You're obviously upset. But right now, I've got people waiting for me. Tell me whatever else you came here to say and go home. I still have a lot of calls to make."

"So glad to know some people get priority status, even if one of them isn't your wife!" She raised her voice loud enough on the last word that Lara overheard.

Morgan ducked his head and reached for Annie's shoulder.

She pulled away.

"If you want to have a rational discussion, Annie, get inside the truck. Otherwise, we're done here."

"That's right, you've got to get back to Miss Powersuit! What is she doing here anyway? Thinking of becoming a volunteer firefighter?"

"That's enough. You're making a scene. Go home, Annie. We can discuss this there."

"So you're actually coming home?"

"Yes," he said, "I'll be home tonight."

"Before or after dinner with her?"

"Why? Making something for dinner besides yogurt?"

Annie glared at him, torn between further making a scene and giving him what he wanted. But if she left, that would leave him there with that woman.

He glanced over his shoulder in the direction of the woman in question, who pointedly checked her watch. Morgan shifted his weight from one hip to the other. "Are we done?"

Annie looked into his dark blue eyes, hoping to see some spark of hope. There was none. She fumed. "Yes and no."

Morgan shook his head. "I don't know what that means." His voice dropped. "I'll be home later and you can explain it to me."

Annie silently watched him walk away from her and towards Lara. She got into her truck and slammed the door. But before pointing her truck away from the fire station, in her mind, she ran over the both of them. She switched off the radio that had distracted her on the way over. Now, the sound of other people's voices grated her nerves.

She drove in silence. Nearing home, she opened her window to listen to the sound of the ocean, hoping to clear her mind of her cheating husband.

Leaving the truck's engine running in the driveway, she popped her head inside the kitchen to check Glenda and the puppies. All were still sleeping.

She would have to walk into the funeral home sometime, might as well be now.

Courage could come from anger.

She'd seen the place enough times, driving past it on her way to her mother's condominium. She'd just never considered needing to go inside until now.

She stared down at the brass urn in her hands. With its two handles, one on either side, it reminded her of a sailing trophy cup. Strange that her mother would pick such a design since she'd never enjoyed sailing once that Annie could recall. Perhaps her mother's choice had something to do with Morgan's love of the sport; she didn't know. She held it at arm's length as she walked and couldn't decide what to do with it once she got into the truck.

Should I hold it between my knees as I drive? No, that would get in the way of the steering wheel. Should I put it in a cup holder? No, the base won't fit.

The plastic milk crate that held some of her office junk still sat in the back of her truck. She hadn't brought it inside when she'd unpacked yesterday. She set the urn carefully on the carpeted floor and shoved the empty manila folders aside to make room for the urn. Her mother had been reduced to being balanced precariously in a crate in the back of her truck. Annie shivered.

This is not my mother.

She tucked the bill from the funeral home inside the crate along with her—it. When she'd seen the cost on the receipt, her eyes had nearly popped out of her head. The cheap and easy way. She removed the yellow piece of paper from the crate and looked at it again. Her mother's insurance would pay for it. She changed her mind and stuffed the receipt into her purse, closing the hatch.

Her mother's condominium, 1111 Ocean Boulevard, had a beautiful view of the ocean. There were plenty of women her mother's age living there and a few men. And she had cut all of their hair. Growing up, Annie's mother had cut her hair too as well as their neighbors and their parents. She made friends wherever she went that way. Annie had envied the time her mother had spent with her friends. Growing up as an only child and with no father, her mother had been all Annie had, besides Bryant. But her mother's work as a beautician had given her regular hours and good money, something that some of her friends' mothers didn't enjoy. The neighbor's children often fell asleep on their living room couch waiting for their mothers to come home after being held up at their jobs. Her mother, Stella Ann Peters, had taken in anyone who needed a soft place to land, one of the things Annie had learned from her.

Once she let herself inside the condo with her spare key, she didn't know exactly what to do. Something told her that her mother would like to be home again. The thermostat dial sat at eighty degrees, the same temperature her mother always kept it.

Annie set the urn down on the coffee table on top of a Marie Clare magazine and opened a window. The sound of the surf filled the two-bedroom condo her mother had lived in all of Annie's life, only a mile from hers and Morgan's house.

Morgan had liked her mother. "I'll never hurt Annie," he had said to her the day they'd married. "I'll keep her safe. You can count on that, Ms. Peters."

They had all stood under a gazebo in the botanical garden behind the zoo, the small reception, firemen and friends of her mother, going on all around them.

"You can call me Stella."

"Okay, Stella. I want you to know that your daughter is more precious to me than anything in this world. And I'm going to do everything I can to make her happy."

Annie now picked out a dish rag from the kitchen drawer, noticing the scars on her hands. She washed the empty popcorn bowl sitting in the sink and dried it. As she put it into the cabinet where it nested with other bowls of various colors, just one of her mother's treasures from the QVC, it occurred to her that it would fall to her to clean out her mother's condo.

She opened the refrigerator. Nothing inside had an expiration date, only twelve ounce Pepsi bottles and an open bag of fun size Snickers. In the kitchen cabinets, one entire drawer held nothing but McDonald's ketchup packets. At least a dozen lottery tickets had been taped to the fridge. Annie pealed them off one by one and tossed them into the trash. As a math teacher she found the whole notion of selling lottery tickets to the unsuspecting, with better odds of getting struck by lightning than winning, offensive. The contents of the fridge and freezer went next, a tub of Cool Whip and a box of fish sticks. The cabinets were in much the same shape. Boxes of cake mix and instant icing, a box of chocolate covered cherries, a can of Cheez Whiz, rice cakes, a small jar of peanut butter, and a jar of maraschino cherries, all went into the trash. There were no spices to speak of, Annie had inherited her mother's lack of talent in the kitchen, just a grocery store set of salt and pepper shakers. But she'd still managed to fill an entire trash can with all she collected.

She made her way into her mother's bedroom next. She steeled herself then opened the closet door only to quickly close it again. Seeing her mother's clothes, hanging there, smelling the perfume that still clung to them, sent a wave of unexpected pain washing over her.

Her mother's desk held stacks of letters and bills. Annie sat down in front of the makeup mirror that occupied a space between the papers and looked at her reflection. Annie wore her hair simply cut in a shoulder length bob. Her mother had worn hers in an elaborate bouffant. Annie didn't think that even her mother remembered the natural color of her own hair, though she'd always dyed it red. Annie's was a dark, reddish brown. Where her mother had a square jaw, Annie's was v-shaped. Her mother had brown eyes; Annie's were blue. Her mother never talked about her father, but Annie had always assumed she'd inherited his looks.

Annie removed the makeup mirror and all of the makeup and perfume bottles from the top of the desk and placed them on the waterbed. The stack of papers on the desk reached almost to the window above. At the top sat a bill from the power company marked past due. She thumbed through the stack and they all said the same thing, past due. Annie's stomach dropped. Her mother didn't own a computer, so everything she did, she did on paper. She'd had no idea of the financial situation her mother had obviously been in. Suddenly, she wanted to talk to Morgan, to hear his voice, but she couldn't. Her heart ached. She didn't want to hear the disappointment in his voice when he answered her call, then the impatience to get off the phone. He would not want to talk to her after what had just happened between them in that parking lot.

She closed her eyes against the headache that formed. She flopped down on her mother's bed and it sloshed beneath her, a wave of water taking her for a ride. She shoved away the four-year-old bottle of Liz Claiborne perfume that Annie had bought for Mother's Day. It rolled towards her again, this time bumping her nose. Tears streamed down her cheeks. Suddenly a little girl again in her mother's room, she saw everything out of proportion, bigger than she, a grown woman.

The doorbell rang.

Annie dragged herself off the bed and trudged to the door, wiping her nose with a tissue from a knitted cozy her mother had made.

Through the peephole, a man with a gray comb-over stood on the front stoop, holding a yellow piece of paper in his right hand. Shorter than Annie, the man wore a pair of neon green running shoes. "I'm Henry Dekaretry," he said, "the condo board president. Are you Stella's daughter?"

"I am."

"I was sorry to hear of your mother's passing.

She was very popular here at Sunny Pines." The last few words were spoken through clenched teeth. He grazed his comb-over with the fingertips of his left hand.

"Mr. Dekaretry, were you here the night my mother died?"

"Yes, I was." The man looked down at his neon green shoes, nodding. "The whole thing was over within minutes."

"You called the paramedics?"

"No, that was Mrs. Vitkevich. She was here visiting your mother when it happened. She mentioned to me that it had been a while since the two of them had seen one another."

"I thought Mrs. Vitkevich lived here at Sunny Pines."

"Not for some time. Her contract was terminated."

"Terminated? What does that mean?"

"Generally speaking, it means that a resident has broken too many rules in a short amount of time, or they've done something bad enough that they're asked to vacate immediately."

"What kind of *bad* things are we talking about?"

"Well, keeping an animal for one. We don't tolerate that kind of thing here."

When he didn't continue, she lifted her brows. "Anything else?"

"Yes," he hesitated, "anything illegal."

"Oh," Annie wrinkled her nose, "is that something that's happened *here*?"

"Well, let's just say that Mrs. Vitkevich's behavior led to the enforcement of the rules."

The way he was talking, Annie imagined a prostitution ring being run out of the older woman's condo. "I have to ask, what did she do?"

"Pets are not allowed at Sunny Pines under any circumstances."

"And Mrs. Vitkevich owned a pet?"

"Not just a pet, a dog."

"Oh, I see." Annie pressed her lips together to keep from smiling. "I happen to know that she was a good person, one of my mother's regulars at the salon."

"Yes, well, I hate to be the bearer of bad news, but Mrs. Vitkevich was not the only resident to have broken our rules. At a time like this, I'm sure you have plenty of things on your mind, but you'll have to learn of this sooner or later. Stella was not a member in good standing with the condo association. Over the last seven years, she's paid only half or in some years only a fraction of the member's dues. To be perfectly honest, there's a lean on her condominium that must be paid before it can be sold."

Annie opened her mouth. She didn't know how to respond.

Who does he think he is, talking about my mother this way?

She had been a generous woman. But what he said must be true; she'd already seen the proof for herself.

"Thank you for bringing this." She took the paper from his hand and started to close the door.

He stuck his head inside to prevent her. "I can take a check right now."

Annie looked down at the piece of paper in her

hand, and he followed her into the living room. Her eyes rounded as she looked at the grand total her mother owed. "Let me find my mother's checkbook."

"I'll wait right here." Henry looked around the living room while Annie went into the bedroom. Her mother always kept her purse in the same place, on top of her chest of drawers. Her hands closed around her mother's checkbook and froze.

Could I go to jail for writing a bad check from her account?

She leafed through the checkbook's record. Instead of seeing checks written to the power company and the water company, there were names of people her mother knew, Betty Vitkevich, Nancy Carlucci, Sarah Greis, and Tabbie Weaver. Annie recognized most of them from all the way back to her childhood. At the bottom of each check, she'd written a note. One said, granddaughter's violin lessons. Another said, son's snow tires. As she flipped through the register, each entry indicated some charitable reason or another. It seemed her mother had been loaning money to her friends. And there was none left.

"Mr. Dekaretry," Annie said, entering the living room, "I'm afraid I'm going to need a little time to go through my mother's finances before I can do anything."

"I understand." He cleared his throat and clasped his hands behind his back, causing his round middle to stick out. "But I'm afraid this will be handed over to a collection agency if I don't receive payment today."

Annie stared at the man in front of her. No taller

than she, yet he appeared to loom over her. "Let me get my purse." She looked inside her own purse she'd left sitting on the sofa and sighed. She'd left her checkbook at home. Then her hand touched the bill from the funeral home. That would fall to Annie as well. Suddenly, her honeymoon plans with Morgan slid away.

"I take credit cards too," Mr. Dekaretry said. He pulled his phone out of his pocket and plugged in a credit card swiper.

"Excuse me, Henry." Mrs. Nancy Carlucci, her mother's next-door neighbor, stuck her head through the open doorway.

Annie had spoken to her several times over the years. Her mother had kept her hair the reddish blond bouffant it was, and Annie had always been impressed by the size of the diamond her second husband had weighed down her ring finger with. She was always one to wear colorful outfits, and today's was no different, a fuchsia and teal rayon track suit. Her acrylic nails were painted pink to match.

"I am so sorry about your mother, dear. I wasn't here when it happened. I hear Betty was. But I want you to know that you have my deepest sympathy."

"Thank you, Mrs. Carlucci."

Henry Dekaretry sighed.

"Mr. Dekaretry and I were just discussing my mother's financial situation. Seems she never paid her association dues."

"No?" Mrs. Carlucci looked around the condo's living room, tilting her head back to try to see into the kitchen. "Your mother was never one to follow rules. She could never stick to her diets."

"I know. But Mrs. Carlucci, can you think of any reason she may have had for not paying? I mean it's not as if she didn't make any money cutting hair. And she never said a thing to Morgan or me."

"Well, she wouldn't have. She didn't think there was anything to tell."

"She has no money in her bank account."

Nancy Carlucci frowned, pausing in her apparent search of the condo on her way into the kitchen.

"Is there anything I can help you with?" Annie said.

The older woman smiled then took a tentative step into the kitchen, glancing at the refrigerator. She frowned.

"Are you looking for something in particular?"

The older woman looked down at her ring finger and fiddled with the diamond there. "Your mother and I went in on some lottery tickets. I hoped she may still have them."

Annie jerked her head back slightly. Mrs. Carlucci cared about lottery tickets? "Of course. They're still here. Let me get them for you." She dug beneath the box of funfetti cake mix and found them. Only one of the ticket's ink had been smudged from being stuck to the tub of frozen cool whip. Annie peeled it off and handed them all to Mrs. Carlucci, who took them with an uneasy smile.

"You're sure you don't mind?"

"I don't put any hope in winning the lottery, so you're welcome to all of them. And I wish you good luck."

"Thank you, dear." Mrs. Carlucci looked at Mr. Dekaretry, who watched her open-mouthed take the lottery tickets from Annie, fold them up, and put them into the pocket of her track suit. "I must be going. I've got a dentist appointment." She turned back to Annie on her way out the front door. "Take care, dear. Your mother loved you very much."

Annie tried to smile at her then watched the older woman walk away, very much wishing her mother were still there to help her understand all of this and to ask her, *why*?

Chapter 5

All the way home, Annie couldn't shake the feeling that there was more to the state of her mother's finances than her generosity getting the better of her. Annie shook her head. She checked again on the new mother and her puppies. Glenda had moved but still lay on her side resting. The babies were all perfectly clean now.

"See? I told you you'd make a great mother."

She carried the dog's water bowl to her, placing it beside her. Glenda did her best to drink without disturbing her puppies. Annie then tried hand-feeding her a few pieces of the dog food. She turned her nose away.

"I can't blame you. If I'd just given birth to five babies, I don't think I'd have much of an appetite either."

Leaving the new family in peace, she promised to check back in about an hour. Glenda winked at her them promptly drifted back to sleep.

Upstairs, Annie opened her laptop. A reply waited for her from the travel agent she'd emailed.

What the heck?

The package deal the travel agent had going right now just happened to be the exact amount Annie had just put on her credit card to pay off her mother's condo president. Her hope for a honeymoon diminished as her savings account dwindled before her very eyes.

An email from Bryant waited for her too. A flicker of happiness passed through her.

"Even though there's an ocean between us I can still feel you standing beside me, hear you move, smell your scent. I miss you, Annie. Maybe the thousands of miles are making me say things I'd never say otherwise, but I don't like going to bed at night knowing that I have to face another day without seeing you and hearing your voice, smelling the apple shampoo you use in your hair. You may be surprised that I noticed, but I did. I always did."

Annie sat frozen, unable to think, to write, to move. A physicist, Bryant lived in his head. He had never been the type to share or even have emotions, except irritation with her when she couldn't see him. But that was Bryant, impatient when he didn't get his way. But this was a different voice speaking for him. She had to chalk it up to homesickness and nothing more, because anything else would scare the life out of her. Bryant didn't have real feelings for her. He couldn't.

She looked at the scars on her hands. Bryant had been there that night. He made a habit of seeing Annie swim at the restaurant. When her crazy ex attacked her, her first thought had been to call him. But he had already gone by then. A very hazy memory of being in the back of the ambulance popped into her head. Her cell phone had rung. Morgan had answered it. She couldn't remember exactly what he'd said, just the gist, something very protective and manly that had warmed her inside. "Annie's been hurt, but she's going to be alright. I'll make sure she's okay. She's safe now."

She had been okay, even bleeding in the back of that ambulance. And not only had she been safe, even in that c-collar with Morgan hovering over her, his breath brushing her cheeks and his eyes looking into hers, she'd been almost peaceful. Everything he'd said, he'd meant. He would make sure she was okay.

Bryant had been at the hospital when she'd awoken. But so had Morgan. Morgan had held a bouquet of red roses. Bryant's face had looked like stone. Then it had just been her and Morgan. He'd come to see her every day, bringing her another bouquet of flowers and with it the promise of his protection. She had taken for granted that Morgan would always be with her, always protect her from ex-boyfriends, always want her. Too much for granted.

A footstep on the threshold of the room, startled Annie. She slammed her laptop shut.

Morgan's eyes narrowed on her face then went to the laptop. "Did I surprise you?"

"Yes, I didn't hear you come in."

"I said I'd be home."

Annie furrowed her eyebrows. "I've heard that before."

"Well, I'm home now." His harsh tone caused her to flinch inwardly.

She stood up from the make-shift desk. "Have you had lunch?"

"No. I'll make something if you're hungry."

Annie's stomach growled as Morgan followed her down the stairs.

"What's this?" Morgan said as they entered the kitchen.

"Didn't you see? Glenda had her puppies. That was one of the things I wanted to tell you this morning."

Morgan turned away from the dog who'd awakened and popped her head up to look at him, a wary look in her eyes.

"What was the other thing you wanted to tell me?" he said, ignoring the dog.

Annie pushed her hair back from her forehead. "I can't remember. After everything that's happened today, I don't know anymore."

"Well, you'll feel better after you get some food in you." Morgan looked her up and down. "Haven't you been eating? You look like you've lost some weight."

His tone sounded critical, not complimentary. Annie looked down at her stomach, her arms, her legs. She hadn't noticed. But there were a lot of things she hadn't noticed, like the fact that her husband may have fallen for another woman.

"What were you doing when I came in?" His voice was deceptively calm.

Annie avoided the topic of Bryant. "Checking my email. I got in touch with a travel agent yesterday. That was the other thing I wanted to tell you."

"Oh? What'd you do that for?" Morgan opened the refrigerator and removed a pink carton of eggs. There were only four inside after the omelets he'd made for them yesterday. He cracked the remaining eggs directly onto the sizzling pan, making fried eggs.

As Annie considered her words, her cheeks heated. Telling him that she wanted a honeymoon would be admitting that she still wanted him. And after all they'd been through, she didn't know how he'd take the news. To buy herself a moment, she went to the toaster and added four slices of whole wheat bread.

"I wanted to take that honeymoon we never had."

Morgan stopped mid-reach for a spatula from the crock beside the stove. "A honeymoon?"

Annie's whole body tensed. She waited for him to say that he couldn't spare the time from his business.

"I thought you didn't want a honeymoon. You said you didn't."

She relaxed her posture a little. "I know I did. But I changed my mind."

After a moment, Morgan spoke. "Sounds good."

"Really? I mean, you want to? You can get away from work for a week?"

"Sure."

Annie let go of the breath she'd held. The past few days had left her drained, emotionally and financially. She had no more to give. "Well, it doesn't matter anymore," she said, her tone flat. "We can't."

"What are you talking about? I just said I wanted to."

"It's the money I had saved—for the college fund, I mean." She peered up at his face beneath her eyelashes. They didn't talk about that subject anymore, hadn't for a long time. She waited for his reaction.

His face remained impassive. Only his lips became a grim line. "Hm, hm."

"I've had to pay off mother's condo dues. Seems she hasn't paid them since we got married."

"What?" He turned from the stove to face her. "When did all of this come about?"

"Today, when I went to her condo."

"Annie, you didn't have to do that alone. I would've gone with you."

"That's another reason I came to see you today. But you couldn't be bothered. I had to pick up her ashes from the funeral home."

Morgan, who'd turned back to the stove, glanced at her quickly, his bright blue eyes dimmed, then glanced away.

"I picked them up and took them to her condo. While I was there, this man, the president of the association came over and said he needed the money right away."

Morgan's brow knit together in a disapproving look.

"He gave me a receipt," she raised her brows at him, "which he signed himself."

Morgan's expression relaxed a little.

"Anyways, she's got no money. There's not even enough to pay me back for the cremation."

"Surely she had life insurance."

"Not unless you count lottery tickets."

"Tomorrow's Saturday. I'll go back there with you and have a look through her papers. There's got to be something stashed away."

They ate in strained silence, and even though she took comfort in sitting down at the table with him and feeling his presence in the house, a part of her wished he would go so that she could swim tonight. He would never approve of her nude night swimming.

After the dishes were packed away in the

dishwasher, she watched the sunset from their living room window. Some sailing race or other blared on the television, garnering all of Morgan's attention between texts on his cell phone. Still no moon had appeared in the night sky. The darkness outside seeped all the way into her bones.

Where will my relief come from tonight?

Not from inside the house and not from swimming. She went to bed unable to relax, uncertain of what time Morgan finally joined her there. And staying to his side of the bed, he lay on his side, facing the wall and fell asleep.

The sun up, Morgan laced his hiking boots. "Take a walk on the beach with me before we go to your mother's." There had been a time when the two of them had taken morning jogs on the beach every weekend. Today, the thought of a whole day indoors inside a stuffy condo made him restless.

Annie shook her head as she brushed her hair, making sure that her scars were covered as she always did. "No, it's too hot."

Morgan walked to her dressing table where she sat looking into the three-way mirror. He admired the curve of her legs, her small waist beneath her shorts, and the natural contour of her breasts. She had the body of a dancer, strong and shapely.

Annie looked up at his reflection as she added a pair of small gold hoops to her earlobes.

Behind her he stood, reflected in the mirror, a white t-shirt covering his flat torso and narrow waist tucked into blue jeans. The rest of him was too tall for the old mirror to capture.

The silken tank top she wore revealed soft skin that begged him to touch it. He reached out for her bare skin, letting his index finger trail across the top of her shoulder.

The contact made Annie's arm convulse reflexively.

Morgan sighed and let his hand drop to his side. He sat down on the trunk at the foot of their bed and watched her slip her feet into a pair of brown sandals. She left their bedroom without a sound.

If she flinched whenever he touched her, then who did she let touch her?

He listened to her walk down the stairs, each creak a step away from him.

When he got to the kitchen, Annie replaced Glenda's water and refilled her food bowl, fussing over the mother-dog's puppies, telling her how cute they were and what a good mother she made.

"They're fine," Morgan said, interrupting her. He picked up his keys and sunglasses from the large shell on the entry way table. "Let's go."

"You don't really want children, do you?"

"What kind of thing is that to say to me right now? We're going to your mother's house to take care of her estate for Christ's sake. Can't we have this argument later?" He slid his sunglasses onto his face so that she could no longer see his eyes.

"You don't even pay any attention to the puppies." She patted Glenda's head, and the dog smiled up at her.

"And you think that means I don't want to have children with you?"

"There has to be a reason we haven't conceived."

Morgan walked to her, placing a hand on either side of her arms, and Annie looked away. "Look at me." He slid his glasses to the top of his head and waited for her to meet his eyes.

She smelled good, like soap and shampoo. When she smelled this way, all the times they'd gone out together came rushing back, dinner, dancing, then returning home as fast as they could to make love wherever they happened to land, on the couch, on their bed if they'd happened to make it that far.

Without turning her head, she cut her eyes to him.

"The doctor told you why we haven't had any kids. It's not your fault or mine."

Annie stood in silence for several breaths.

He could tell she'd closed herself off to him once more. Instead of arguing, he let his hands fall from her shoulders. "Let's go."

Annie tried the key in the brass door lock once more. The morning sun beat down on her back. "It's not turning." Every nerve inside her was raw.

Morgan took the key from her hand and twisted it a few more times.

Annie looked down at the rose bushes beside the front door. Her mother had loved their pink petals surrounding a yellow golden center. One of the green leaves had turned yellow, sending a baseless shaft of fear through Annie.

"Who's going to take care of her roses?"

Waves of pain washed over her like the ocean tide, beating her until she couldn't breathe. Even being consciously aware that her reaction was irrational didn't stop the spiral, all over some roses.

Morgan blew out a breath, completely unaware of Annie's emotional meltdown. "The key doesn't fit. What's the name of the condo president?"

Annie stifled her tears, catching her breath and feeling ridiculous. "Mr. Dekaretry."

"I'm going to find him. I'll be right back."

Annie watched Morgan's retreating figure walk to the condominium's office door, disappearing inside. His gait told her that he'd reached the end of his patience, her doing. Her intention had not been to start an argument, to begin this day of all days on a bad foot. It had been so long since he'd volunteered to spend any time with her, let alone the whole day. His Saturdays off-duty consisted of pouring over emails and paperwork for his business.

She scooted closer to the door to her mother's condo. A gutter overhang provided a sliver of shade on the white pavement. Her mother's unit sat tucked into the left corner of the courtyard that surrounded the office building. The ocean view condos at the front of the complex cost considerably more than the ones at the back. And her mother obviously hadn't been able to afford it and her charity work at the same time. All of those checks made out to her friends for different reasons still nagged at Annie.

Morgan returned moments later with Mr. Dekaretry, who did not look pleased, trailing behind him. He wiped his mouth with a paper napkin. Apparently, Morgan had caught him during his lunch, although it was only ten thirty. But not many people could say no to Morgan, especially in his business-mode.

"Ah, Annie," Mr. Dekaretry said when he spotted her, "it's like I told your husband, the locks have been changed."

"Why?" Morgan asked with no attempt at courtesy.

"Security reasons."

"I need to get into my mother's condo," Annie said. "All of her belongings are still inside."

"No problem. Just come find me whenever you need to get in."

Morgan cleared his throat. "It would be easier on everybody if you gave my wife a copy of that key in your hand."

Mr. Dekaretry looked from the key to Morgan, ready to argue, but Morgan's tone brooked no disagreement and he relented with a sigh. "Yes, I can do that. But just temporarily. I'll expect you to return the key to me as soon as you're finished. The board will want to put the condo on the market by the end of the month."

Annie thanked Mr. Dekaretry for the key and Morgan let them in.

Morgan looked around the living room and small kitchen. "He can have his damn key back by the end of the day. This won't take long to clear out."

"I don't know about that. We can't just throw everything to the curb."

"Why not? Do you want to keep any of this?"

"No. I don't know. Some of it."

Morgan shrugged his broad shoulders. "You said she kept her papers in the bedroom?"

Annie noddcd.

"You look through all this stuff in here, and I'll

look for the insurance paperwork."

On his way past her, he turned the thermostat dial down to sixty-eight degrees.

Annie stood before a bookshelf and looked up and down. Her hand closed over a gray porcelain elephant. Annie recalled the spring break she had spent with her classmates at the elephant sanctuary in Tennessee. When her mother came to pick her up on the last day, they'd stopped in the gift shop and found it.

"An elephant never forgets," her mother had said on the drive back to St. Michaels. "If you were to go back to the sanctuary next year, they would remember you."

And no matter what she had to do, Annie vowed now she would never let herself forget. She would find out why her mother really died and why she died penniless.

Morgan thumbed through the checkbook. Annie had been right; it didn't take a math teacher to see that her mother was broke. The stacks of papers on her desk were surprisingly orderly, utility bills on top, credit card bills, college loan bills below that, then bank statements. Morgan raised his eyebrows as he picked up the bill from UWF. Stella had still been paying off Annie's college tuition. He thumbed through the rest, but no insurance policy was among them.

Morgan opened the closet, hoping to find a filing cabinet tucked away behind the floral muumuus. Nothing. Then he saw it, a small, square safe, about a foot wide and half as tall, hidden beneath a stack of shoe boxes.

If he'd observed anything about older women, and he had had plenty of experience with them on medical calls, taking them to the hospital, they never left home without the key to everything they owned. He found her key ring inside her purse. Behind her Subaru key hung a small key with a round tip.

Inside the safe at the top of a stack of papers sat a pearl handled revolver, loaded. He carefully placed it inside the top drawer of the dresser. Annie's birth certificate lay on top. March 22. Only a few weeks away. No father's name. Stella had given her daughter her own last name, Peters. Beneath Annie's sat Stella's own birth certificate, then Annie's letter of acceptance to the University of West Florida, Stella's cosmetology certificate, the deed to The Solar Day Spa, and at the bottom of them all sat a newspaper clipping. Morgan unfolded the brown and brittle paper.

Former University of West Florida Student Dies in Libya.

The caption beneath a picture of a young man, who bore a striking similarity to Annie with dark hair and light eyes, read Lieutenant Andrew Nathaniel Lipscomb. Annie's dad.

She'd never said a thing about him except that she'd never met him.

This explained a lot. Morgan had always presumed that a woman left alone with a baby to raise on her own would eventually become bitter. But Stella had never said a bad word about him or any other man for that matter. She obviously forgave him for leaving her—he hadn't had a choice.

The stack of papers hid a ten-year-old bottle of Port. Morgan held it in his hand, weighing the possibilities.

He found Annie in the living room, sitting cross-legged on the carpet, surrounded by hardback books, every book Reader's Digest had ever printed.

"Any luck?" she said, looking up at him, her pale blue eyes reminding him of the night at his old apartment he'd made dinner for the two of them. He'd cleaned the place from ceiling to floor, bought new towels, even a freaking candle, set the table with a tablecloth, and made chicken breasts, saffron rice, and mixed vegetables. Not gourmet, but it had impressed.

She'd been in college then and he already a career firefighter. He would spend the rest of his life with her; that had been clear to him all the way back to the day they'd met. When he'd looked into her eyes for the first time inside that ambulance, he'd recognized her. It had slammed into his chest like a freight train. He couldn't explain it, but he had known her and that they'd been thrust together for a reason—he was to spend the rest of his life protecting her.

He didn't have the heart now to tell Annie the things he'd discovered, that her mother had spent most of her income sending her daughter to college and that her father had died before her birth.

Morgan held up the bottle of sweet wine for her to see. "What do you say? Have a drink with me."

Annie frowned and bit her lower lip.

"Your mother wouldn't have wanted it to go to waste."

A slight smile appeared on Annie's face. "That's true."

Morgan followed her into the kitchen where he reached around her to the top shelf for two wine glasses. Annie rinsed the dust from them while Morgan removed the foil from the bottle's neck.

On his fifth glass of Port, Annie's third, Morgan poured a little more into each glass. Without food in his stomach, he found it hard to remember why things were the way they were between them. He wanted Annie every time he looked at her. Sometimes so much that it hurt.

Annie sat on her mother's couch, giggling to herself.

"What's so funny?"

"Remember that night we went to the movies to see that gladiator movie you wanted to see?"

"You're going to have to be a lot more specific than that." Morgan sat down closer to Annie than she usually let him without scooting away. He put his arm around her. She smelled good.

"Oh, you remember. It was sold out when we finally got up to the window. So we had to buy tickets for the next showing."

"Vaguely." Morgan chuckled softly, enjoying seeing her like this. He eased back into the couch and spread his knees apart so that his leg brushed Annie's knee. "Tell me more."

"Well, since we had a half hour to kill, we drove to the drug store for sour cherry balls. I had forgotten that I was out of birth control pills until we walked in. You volunteered to look for the candy while I got my prescription refilled. But the pharmacist was new; he didn't know I was married, and he hit on me. By the time he got around to asking me out, you were standing right behind me." Annie laughed hard now. "When I turned around, your face was so red I thought you were going to burst a blood vessel. I'd never seen you so mad before."

"What do you expect, Annie? I'm your husband. The minute my back is turned, some guy in a lab coat sees you're on the pill and thinks he's found himself an easy score."

"You called him every name in the book. Some I'd never heard before."

"It was worth getting thrown out." Morgan scowled.

"Yeah, but we never got our cherry sour balls and had to eat popcorn without any candy." She pouted her lower lip. "I never did get back on the pill after that night." She stopped laughing.

The memory of how long it had been that they'd not conceived hurt, he knew. Her desire to have a baby and not being able to have one had become an obsession, one he'd been helpless to prevent.

Morgan gently tucked a strand of stray hair behind her ear. "You look lost in thought."

"That night." She smiled. "That was so like you, defender of the weak and the innocent, everything that's yours really."

"You're not weak." Morgan poured two more glasses of the port and returned the bottle to the coffee table in front of them. "But I couldn't let him get away with hitting on you right in front of me. I've got my pride. And you're right, I am protective of everything that's mine." He looked at her, breath streaming from his nostrils. "That's why I can't stand knowing you're with Bryant every time I leave the house."

Annie chuckled. "You make it sound clandestine. He and I are friends. You know that. And you always know when I'm with him."

"Yeah, but do you know how many times I've taken calls from buddies of mine who've seen you two out together, wanting to let me know they saw you with another man?" He raked a hand over his short hair. "It's embarrassing."

"I didn't think anything embarrassed you." She laughed. "But it's funny, you know, I haven't gotten a call from any of them to let me know when you're out with Miss Powersuit. Loyalty only goes one way, I guess."

Morgan heaved a sigh. "Do we have to talk about this right now?"

"No." Annie relaxed into the sofa's cushions, warm and pliant.

"There's no life insurance on your mother." Morgan let out a breath when he'd finished his sentence, just saying it out loud had been difficult.

Annie sucked in a breath. "Okay," she exhaled, "we won't be able to take that honeymoon after all."

His large hand took her face and held it gently. "We don't need to go away to be together."

The underlying sensuality of his words captivated her. Annie's pale blue eyes rounded and a flush of pink tinged her cheeks.

Morgan encircled her waist with his strong arms and kissed her cheek, looking her over seductively. When she didn't pull away, he pulled her body close to his, inhaling the sweet scent of her hair. "I've missed you, Annie."

"Oh, Morgan, I've missed you too."

He kissed her lips tentatively at first until she opened to him. Gently he eased her down on the couch. He placed a hand on either side of the cushions and drew himself over her, placing his knees between her legs. Stretching their bodies out so that he hovered over her, he took his weight with his elbows and knees. He held her cheeks in his palms and kissed her deeply, remembering how it had once been between them, making love at the drop of a hat, laughing, talking, looking into each other's eyes and drifting off to sleep in each other's arms. Now it hurt to even lie down next to her in their bed, knowing that his touch was unwelcome.

Annie wrapped her arms around his neck now and drew him closer. His body responded quickly and desperately like a starving man being offered a seven course meal. He wanted it all and he wanted it fast. He pulled her tank top over her head, allowing his bloodshot eyes to feast on the way her breasts looked inside the lace that surrounded them, the way they moved when he touched them. And of course, there were the scars. As he kissed her neck, he kissed each one of them as he'd always done, letting her know that even though the scars were there, she was beautiful and whole.

He moved to her shorts, unzipping them and pulling them down her legs, letting his fingertips graze her soft skin. His gaze dropped from her eyes to her shoulders to her breasts. She was perfect. As she lay there, one hand behind her head, one hand around his neck, he allowed his eyes to drink her in, finer than any aged Port could ever be.

He removed his own clothes and she clung to him now, naked and desperate for what only he could give her. He knew her body as well as she did and it ached for his touch. His fingers left a trail of heat in their wake as they found her core. The memory of all those nights spent naked, lying in their bed together, returned.

Their bodies fit together perfectly as though made for one another. She caressed the strong muscles of his back. His hands found her pleasure points. Their breaths came heavy as their bodies entwined, holding each other in the perfect rhythm they made. And when they cried out, it was the other's name on their lips as waves of ecstasy throbbed through them. Her body melted against his and the world was made right again.

Morgan smoothed a lock of her hair back from where it had clung to her flushed cheek, gazing at her in quiet admiration. He cupped her cheeks with his palms. His deep voice barely above a whisper filled the quiet. "You're so beautiful, Annie."

She smiled up at him, her eyelids heavy. Relief washed over her. His touch hadn't sent shock waves of dread through her, reminding her of the terrifying night she'd been held down by that monster on the pavement. She had tried not to let herself think about the past. And when the memories came unbidden as they did, the rightness of being with Morgan overcame them. In the comfort of the sofa, a placid drowsiness overtook her muscles, even reaching her bones. She couldn't keep her eyes open.

When she awakened, it was well past lunchtime.

But with no food in the condo, they were out of luck. Morgan slept on his side next to her still. She'd half expected him to be back on his phone by now. But there he was, lying face to face with her. She couldn't resist staring at his strong jaw, his muscular shoulders, the dips and valleys in his abdomen, the way his breath caused his chest muscles to move up and down. And further down, she looked to the place where his flat stomach became a dark patch of curls. Morgan was all man and sometimes too much for her. She wondered again how she'd gotten so lucky. How does a man, who could have any woman of his choosing, pick her?

Like a child at play, she used the tip of her index finger to trace the lines of his mouth and smiled to herself.

He opened his eyes slowly to find her watching him. Through the haze of sleep and good Port, his voice was gravelly from sleep. "Lonely?" He grinned.

"Not anymore."

With one arm wrapped around her waist, he pulled her even closer to him, inhaling deeply as he did, relaxing into the curves of her body.

She reveled in this moment, connection with Morgan, finding their way back to one another. Possibly they could become friends again like they had been once, laughing easily instead of stilted silence.

Morgan's cell phone rang, breaking the spell, sending her crashing back down to reality. Work. Lara. Betrayal. Loneliness.

From her prone position, Annie looked down at the phone's display before Morgan had a chance to answer it.

"Lara." Her voice held all the contempt she felt for that name. Reality had shattered the moment, taking with it all hope of returning to wedded bliss.

"Annie..." Morgan sat up.

Annie did too, covering her naked breasts with her arms. "What a surprise. I'm shocked that it took her this long to call you today."

"Annie..." Morgan reached for her arm.

She dodged his hand. "Annie, what? Annie, don't be jealous. Annie, don't be a shrew. Annie, can't we just call a truce? I know. I've heard all of those things from you before. And do you want to know what I think?"

Torn between answering Annie and answering his phone, Morgan remained silent.

Instead of answering her own question, she shrieked, a high-pitched cry that started in her abdomen and came up through her throat like a moan, not nearly as loud as she'd needed it to be.

"Keep your voice down. There are neighbors who can hear you."

"And you think I care about that?" She wouldn't apologize; it had felt too good to let it out finally. "Go ahead, answer your phone."

Morgan stood, pulling on his boxer briefs and jeans. "It's too late. It's gone to voice mail."

"Too bad." Annie gave him a pouting look, and he glared back at her. Then he seemed to think better of it. He pulled his white t-shirt over his head and his expression had softened. He grabbed her arm, but she pulled away. He held tighter.

"I knew it was too good to be true."

Morgan released her arm and turned away. His expression returned to the vacant look she'd become so accustomed to.

"What is that supposed to mean?" she said, but she didn't have to ask. Whatever resolve for peace that had been between them had evaporated.

"It means that I'm not allowed to touch you unless there's alcohol involved."

Annie watched Morgan open-mouthed lace up his boots. Finally, he looked at the mess of books and knick-knacks in the center of the room. "Let's go. I've got work to do. I'll pick up some boxes after work tomorrow so we can pack up this junk."

Annie pulled her tank top over her head and stepped into her shorts. Dressed, she hurriedly looked around the room. The ceramic elephant still sat on the bookshelf with the other knick-knacks. She tucked the elephant inside her purse. She didn't know why, but something compelled her to keep it.

Chapter 6

At home, the silence between them hung heavily.

Annie found a place on her bedside table for the little gray elephant next to the gray conch shell. She listened to Morgan answer phone messages. When she couldn't hear his deep voice drifting up the stairs she knew he'd started texting, then he'd get back on the phone and she'd listen to the timbre of his voice once again. She didn't know which hurt her more, him being away from home or him being at home and so far from her.

She flopped down on the steamer trunk at the foot of their bed. An apple red throw lay across its top, the fleece tickling the backs of her knees until she stood and turned. It had been years since she'd looked inside the trunk. She knelt. With both hands lifting its large lid, careful not to slice her hand on the broken brass lock that had been cut years before when the key was lost, she peered inside. Like a staircase, levels of shelves opened. On its top shelf sat an antique wooden box with roses inlaid in the cover. Inside were the dried petals from the bouquet of twelve red roses Morgan had given her in the hospital, one for every month of the year he said he wanted to spend with her for the rest of his life.

She'd been in the hospital bed still recovering when he'd proposed to her. Her mother had obviously been in on it because she'd insisted Annie wash her hair and put on a little makeup before Morgan arrived that day. She'd always known when to expect him back then. Like clockwork, he'd be there as soon as his shifts ended. He'd arrived that particular day holding the bouquet and wearing a funny expression on his face. She half expected a camera crew to appear behind him and hear people laughing. But then he'd gotten down on one knee, not an easy thing to do beside a hospital bed. And her whole world had changed.

"Annie, you've shown me how incomplete my life has been without you in it. Now that you are, I don't want another day to pass without knowing that you always will be. Spend the rest of your life with me? Marry me?"

Heart-felt and to the point, like Morgan. And she'd said all she could say through the lump in her throat, "Yes."

She sat back on the floor now and hugged her arms around her knees, rocking gently. That had been the Morgan she'd fallen in love with, not this Morgan, secretive with his phone, completely distracted by work, and always vacant at home.

Her email. She hadn't checked it that morning. The last time Bryant went out of town, he'd met Candace and married her, a woman he'd known for only three days. And since Annie had refused to go to Italy with him, there was no telling what he might do this time.

She'd emailed him all about Glenda and her puppies. She'd said that the birth had gone remarkably well, though Glenda had done all the work, and how ridiculously jealous she was of a dog for becoming a mother when she couldn't.

"You're going to make a great mother to some very lucky kids someday," his email said.

Annie smiled as she read the first line.

"Annie, I know I've said this already in the past two days, but I'll say it again. Maybe it's the ocean separating us, but I miss you like crazy. I go to bed thinking about you. I wake up and you're the first thought in my head."

A surge of adrenaline hit her. How was she supposed to take this new Bryant? He had always been moody, until he'd asked her to go away with him. Now he'd become a different person, speaking with a different voice.

"It's always been you, Annie. You're in my heart. You're in my head. Every woman I've ever taken to my bed has been you. That's why my wife left me. She said I was in love with you and she couldn't stand being second to any other woman. And she was right. I was in love with you, Annie."

Annie shook her head. Her hands shook too hard to write a reply, not that she had one. She got up from the rocking chair, backing away from the dresser and the open laptop as if it could somehow read her thoughts. She had to get away.

The sound of the backdoor opening and closing caught Morgan's attention from the living room. Annie must have gone out into the backyard. He had more work to do, but he couldn't see straight anymore from staring too long at the screen on his laptop and phone. He stood and stretched. The sun set on the horizon and a jog on the sand sounded like just what he needed now.

He gathered his papers, computer, phone, and charging cords and carried them all upstairs to his duffel bag that served as his portable office. He would look at them again tomorrow during his downtime on duty. Now that he and Annie had cooled off, they had some things to discuss. He just needed a run to gather his thoughts. After that, he could talk. On his way out of their bedroom, running shoes in hand, Morgan passed the room that would've one day been the nursery. Annie's words that morning ran through his mind. "You don't really want children, do you?"

He had nothing against having kids of their own. Fear held him back. It had taken him seven years of marriage to be able to even admit that to himself, let alone to Annie. She still didn't know. Being a father, being responsible for another human life scared him especially after losing his father the way he had. She had been right; he hadn't paid any attention to the puppies. Every time he walked into the kitchen for a drink or for food from the refrigerator, he avoided even looking in their direction. So small, so delicate. He of all people had a firm grasp of how precious life was, how strong yet fragile the body could be. He didn't need reminders around him to be constantly aware of that fact, a life could end without a moment's notice. Every time Annie's pale bloodied face in that ambulance popped into his head, he felt like he'd taken a punch to his gut. The thought of looking down into the eyes of a little girl who looked just like her made his chest constrict the way it did when he gave speeches at work. He couldn't breathe.

He looked around the room now. Annie had removed everything she'd bought for the nursery.

Everything that would have one day belonged to their baby was gone. Only the wallpaper with the gray elephants walking in a line remained, the baby elephant using its trunk to hold onto its mother's tail. The space felt wrong. A rocking chair faced the dresser that would have doubled as their changing table. Annie had had to explain to him how that would work. "We'll attach this concave cushion to the top of the dresser. The baby will lay here. And that's how we'll change diapers. All the supplies stay in here." She had opened the top dresser drawer and shown him the container of baby wipes and diaper rash ointment inside.

Morgan open the drawer now. Those things were still there, which gave him a modicum of comfort. Annie giving up on having a child was somehow equivalent to her giving up on him. And he wasn't going to let her do that.

Her laptop sat on top of the dresser. She'd left the screen open to her email.

Bryant Smith. The man's name stood out like a flashing neon sign.

Morgan's heart began to pound in his chest. He shouldn't read it. As he scrolled down the screen, a voice in his head said he shouldn't violate her trust. But he had to know. Annie was his.

"I am in love with you, Annie, and I think you know it. I think you've always known." Bryant's words stabbed into Morgan like a knife to his back.

Morgan slammed the laptop's lid shut and backed out of the room, the words written by that man to his wife still echoing in his mind.

Annie walked along the beach, carrying her canvas flip flops, letting the wet sand squish between her toes. The sun had completely set and had taken with it its unrelenting glare. With no heat beating down on her skin, she could think clearly, she could reason. Bryant had to be told something. What? She didn't know. How could she tell the man who'd been there for her since she'd turned thirteen years old that she didn't love him back, at least not in the way he obviously did? She could still see him on his skateboard in her driveway, hear him coughing because he'd taken up smoking, smell the cigarettes on his breath, feel the cold concrete curb beneath her thighs as they waited for the bus together before school.

Her mother would tell her to just come right out with it. "No sense beating around the bush." She never had. If she hadn't liked a person, she'd tell them.

"You're not from around here," her mother had said to Bryant when they'd first met, frowning as she crossed her arms over her chest, looking him up and down. Not like Morgan.

"I like you," she'd said to him at their first meeting.

Of course, she'd credited him with saving her daughter's life. So in her mother's eyes, Morgan could do no wrong. Whenever she'd come across an extra ticket to a game, she'd given it to Morgan. Whenever she'd baked a cake, it had been for Morgan. If she'd ever had a question about something, anything, she'd asked Morgan—except her finances. Those she'd kept to herself.

"I'm sorry, Bryant, that I can't return your

feelings. I'll always love you..." As a friend? That sounded like something she would've said to him back in middle school if he had professed his love for her then. Had he gotten it over with then, she wouldn't be in this predicament now.

Back inside the house now, the muscles in Annie's shoulders relaxed. She checked in on Glenda and saw that the puppies had opened their eyes. They were all in the same spot she'd left them, but things were already changing. One girl puppy looked just like her mother. She'd call her Little Glenda for now. She stroked her silky head. One of the boys, she'd call Petey, must have taken after his father because he had brown hair and a white spot on one ear. The other two boys were the same color beige as their mother, one she named Benji and the other Blue. The second girl looked like her father as well, so she named her Tabitha.

Annie pictured a little girl that took after Morgan, tall with dark hair and dark blue eyes, gorgeous. Suddenly, looking at Glenda's little family, Annie's dream inched closer to reality.

She called out for Morgan but got no answer. The house was too quiet. As she walked through the living room, she could see that his keys and sunglasses were no longer in their usual place by the front door in the shell. Her heart jumped into her throat. She continued to call as she took each creaky wooden step upstairs. From the top of the landing through their open bedroom door, she could see that he was not there either. Passing the open nursery door, she glanced inside. Her laptop. She'd left it open. It was closed now.

Bryant's email had been the last thing she'd read.

Morgan had seen it, read it, and assumed there was something between her and Bryant.

In the bedroom, his duffel bag was gone. His t-shirts, shorts, and socks were missing from his highboy. His uniform shirts and pants were not on his side of the closet. Not even his shoes were there. His phone was gone too.

Morgan opened Stella's condominium with the key he'd taken from Annie's purse. The cool air rushed to him, unlike all the other times he'd been inside the condo over the years. He set down his two duffel bags, one for work and one full of clothes. He would sleep on the couch tonight.

He went back to his truck for the empty boxes. He'd called a firefighter buddy of his who worked part-time at an industrial supply company. He'd set the boxes aside for Morgan, who now dropped the bundle of flattened cardboard in the middle of the living room floor and got to work shaping the boxes. He might as well do something productive with his Saturday evening since he wouldn't be spending it with his wife as he'd hoped. Two hours later, the contents of the place were safely tucked inside four large shipping boxes. Morgan loaded them onto his truck and drove to Goodwill.

Annie sat slumped in the rocking chair, rereading Bryant's email over and over again, punishing herself for not deleting it, for not realizing sooner that their relationship had become what it had. Because of it, she'd lost the one man she did love, the only man she'd ever truly loved.

She watched the cursor blink. Her fingers poised over the keyboard, she planned how she would tell Bryant that she couldn't continue their relationship.

"I hope all is well there." She hit send and waited. Internet reception there must be good because in moments she had an answer.

"Since you didn't reply to my message, I assume I know why. You don't return my feelings. What was I thinking? You're married to your dream prince. I'm a frog. Disregard everything that I said. I was homesick. That's what I'm telling myself."

"Morgan has moved out." She hit send.

"Do you want me to come home?"

What?

"No," she typed, "this opportunity is too important to your career."

"Annie, don't be brave. You've been through the wringer with your mother dying and now Morgan abandons you in your moment of need."

"I'm fine. I've got the puppies to keep me busy."

Not to mention going crazy wondering why my mother's bank account was empty. I wouldn't even have known if she hadn't died.

"I really think I should come home. The university will understand. And you and I can go back to the way things were."

"I've quit my job at the university."

No reply came.

Annie stared at the blank screen. She let a few minutes pass in silence, watching the cursor blink. Finally, she gave up and drifted downstairs to check on the puppies. She found Glenda sleeping soundly and with five puppies wiggling all around her, that was saying something.

After forcing a cup of yogurt down for her dinner, Annie went back upstairs.

Still no reply from Bryant.

She showered and changed into a pair of silk pajamas, but when she laid down on her bed, the spaghetti straps dug into her shoulders. The waistband of the shorts twisted when she rolled over. She sighed, turning over on her side, propping her head up on one hand to look out the window. There was no visible moon yet again tonight.

Annie knew she wouldn't find sleep, not until she allowed her mind to sift through her mother's death. She slipped out of bed, ignoring the laptop sitting on the nursery's dresser. Instead she reached into the back of the closet for a white posterboard she'd brought home from the university. It had been a visual aid she'd made for her first year Geometry students so they could use it on test days, every formula for area and perimeter of every polygon as well as circle. She flipped it over now to its blank side and hung it on the wall with Scotch tape. Down the center of the board, she drew a line, bisecting it across the top so that she'd formed a large, lower case t. At the top left she wrote Knowns, and on the right, she wrote, Unknowns. Under Knowns, she wrote her mother's name, Stella Ann Peters, the date she died, March 2, of apparent heart attack, no insurance, checks written to friends. Beneath her mother's name she wrote her father's name, Lieutenant Andrew Nathaniel Lipscomb. Beneath that, she wrote her mother's friend's names, Tabbie Weaver, Nancy

Carlucci, Betty Vitkevich, Sarah Greis, and Henry Dekaretry. Beneath the Unknowns column, she wrote, cause of death?

Too late for an autopsy.

Would the bank know if her mother had made payments to an insurance company?

Then next to each of their names, she wrote a question mark. She didn't really know these people. Some of them probably had deep, dark secrets.

Before she finished, she also wrote Bryant Smith's name, not that she suspected him of murder, but because his mother hadn't liked him. She took a step back from her chart, horrified by the dark turn her life had taken, but feeling an odd sense of satisfaction from her work. Tomorrow she had to question every one of these people, people she would've trusted yesterday. But for now, she had to escape her troubling thoughts. Especially tonight she needed to swim.

She crept down the stairs so she wouldn't disturb Glenda and slipped out the back door.

No lights on her neighbor's porches meant she didn't have to worry that any of them would see her. She abandoned her clothes on the dry sand next to the dunes and picked her way to the water.

As she dove, she pressed, farther and farther, pushing her lungs past the point of discomfort so that finally when she surfaced, she gasped then went back under to do it all over again. She dove and swam, dove and swam, for how long, she didn't know.

How far could I push myself?

When she next surfaced, she turned back to look

for her house. She had gone past the point where the waves break before shore, farther than she'd ever gone before alone. She shivered as she floated in the immense darkness around her. Her view of the houses on the shore became twisted and odd, like a fun house mirror, and the volume of the waves increased until she covered her ears. Her thoughts crowded together, punishing her for going so far. She questioned her own safety now as she'd never done before. Panic crept into the edges of her mind until her heart pounded. A sudden urgency to return to shore overwhelmed her. As she lifted her arms out of the water with each breaststroke, her hands shook with the effort it took to move the water. With each breath she strained to return to the safety of the shore before her strength gave out completely, before it was too late.

Mere yards became miles. Minutes stretched out to an eternity until finally the sand brushed the tips of her toes once again and she could take a deep breath. She pushed through the remaining water as fast as she could, half-walking, half-swimming, letting the tide take her onto shore with it until the water reached her knees, her ankles, and finally the bottoms of her feet chafed against the wet grains of sand below her. As she took the last step out of the water, she lost her balance on the shifting sand and fell. Her forehead hit the sand, her arms too tired to prevent it. She struggled to her feet, sensing that her panic had to have come from somewhere; something must be terribly wrong at home. Glenda. She snatched up her pajamas, stepping into the shorts as fast as she could. Then, running as she did, she pulled the top over her head.

She reached the back door at a dead run, yanking the brass knob and flinging the door out of her way. Her eyes scanned the kitchen quickly. Glenda and her puppies remained in the safety of their bed right where they were supposed to be. Glenda had not moved. She ran to the bottom of the stairs.

"Morgan!"

No answer. He still wasn't home.

She ran up the steps two at a time, each wooden board complaining beneath her weight until she reached the landing. Inside the old nursery she yanked open the laptop.

Nothing. Still no reply from Bryant.

All alone with her thoughts she recalled the food she'd left in Glenda's bowl that morning. It had not been touched.

A hollow settled in the pit of her stomach. Without wanting to, she took the stairs slowly, each step an agony. She couldn't look. She didn't want to know what waited for her in the kitchen on that brand new baby blue dog bed. She stopped at the edge of the kitchen's threshold, holding her breath, unable to take those final steps inside.

The puppies nursed. Glenda lay peacefully on her side, unmoving. She looked asleep, so innocent, so pure. The pit that had formed in Annie's stomach widened to a gaping hole. She forced herself closer until she could reach out to her dog. She tried, but her hand shook so much, she feared that if she did touch her, and Glenda really did only sleep, she would frighten her. So Annie crouched there, her own heart beating against her thigh, her breaths coming in and out quickly.

Glenda's side did not move. She hadn't moved since Annie had left to go out to the beach. She hadn't stirred when Annie had burst into the kitchen.

"Glenda is an old dog," the vet had said.

Finally, Annie reached out a hand that didn't shake and touched Glenda. Her fingers pressed until she found Glenda's body still warm. But when Annie's hands found their way to Glenda's chest, no heartbeat met her, no sign of life besides the puppies who didn't know their mother, their source of food, of comfort, of safety, their anchor in this world like hers had vanished.

Annie's feet collapsed beneath her and she toppled onto her side beside the dog's bed. A single tear escaped and fell onto her hand that covered her mouth, stifling a moan. She curled her body into a ball as wracking sobs overtook her. Her lungs cried out her grief and her heart broke along with all hope she'd clung to up til then.

Her family. Her belonging. All was lost.

After removing his t-shirt, Morgan stretched out on the sofa in his mother-in-law's living room. The furniture would have to be removed another day. He'd had it. He lay there on his back in his blue jeans and bare feet, one arm beneath his head, exhausted. A list of things waited to be done the following day. Tonight though, all of his energy had been spent packing the house. Any other day and it would have been a cake walk, but not today. His mind wouldn't stop going over the email he'd read. And it asked him the same question over and over. If Annie left that email open, knowing he might stumble upon it, what kind of emails had she hidden from him?

His phone rang just his eyes closed. His forearm draped over his brow didn't move. Forced to check the caller ID by the incessant ringing, it was Lara.

"I can't tell you how many slim-line airpacks I've got in stock right now," he said into the phone. "I'm away from home. I'll call you back on Monday."

He pressed end call and closed his eyes once more.

The phone rang again. Annie's ring. He didn't have the strength for another argument over Lara or Bryant.

He waited for the phone to stop ringing. His mind began to drift, but he held onto consciousness, waiting to hear if she left a voice message.

He didn't know how much time had passed when a firm knock on the door startled him awake. If it was that condo president there to tell him to clear out, the man would regret it. Before opening the door, Morgan reached inside his duffel bag. Just in case it wasn't Dekaretry, he removed his Kahr PM40 and shoved it into the back of his jean's waistband, the cold metal against his bare back.

He could see through the peep hole that it wasn't the old man or his own wife come looking for him. Though part of him had hoped it would be Annie, ready now to have it out with her now. His body stiffened in response. Even angry at her, he still wanted her, the soft curves of her body, the place at the hollow of her throat that made her laugh when he kissed her there, the crease of her outer thigh that drove him wild, and the way she said his name when she reached her completion. She was his.

Lara. She stood on the door's stoop. Her painted lips grinning a crooked grin.

He didn't smile or welcome her. Not this time. "What do you want?"

"Well, I'm happy to see you too." Lara looked him up and down, assessing his bare feet all the way up to his broad shoulders, pausing to linger just below the waistband of his jeans.

He lifted his t-shirt from the back of the chair and slid it over his head, letting the hem hang loose, hiding his taut waist.

"I told you I can't give you any numbers right now." He leaned an elbow against the door's frame.

"I don't need numbers." She walked right past him into the living room. "I need your signature on a new agreement. Richard, says he wants it instated Monday morning, no later. So that means I had to come to you." She sat down on the couch and looked up at him, her brows lifted expectantly.

Morgan frowned. "How did you manage to find me here?"

"You've obviously got location services enabled on your phone or I wouldn't have been able to, now would I? Plus, your truck's parked outside. There aren't a whole lot of those trucks in the city."

Morgan silently cursed. He'd turned on location services on his phone for a training exercise at the fire department and forgotten to turn it off. That meant Annie could also see where he was from her phone. But she hadn't come after him the way Lara had or possibly didn't know to. He didn't like this aggressive streak in Lara. He preferred Annie's feminine approach, even fighting mad. Her eyes had sparked fire when he'd held her arm in that very room earlier in the day. Being overpowered had angered her, but he'd panicked. He couldn't stomach the thought of losing her.

"Can we get this over with?" Morgan's impatient voice now was made all the more abrupt by his increasing concern for his wife. He shouldn't have walked out of the house.

"You tell me." Lara handed Morgan a sheaf of papers bound in a manila folder with a rubber band around them.

He took them from her and arched a brow as Lara removed her fitted suit jacket, revealing a red silk top with spaghetti straps. "Make yourself at home," he said, his tone a long drawl that would've signified with anyone who knew him.

As he took a seat on the opposite end of the couch, she watched Morgan remove the gun from his waist. He could feel her eyes on him as he set it on the coffee table.

"You weren't going to shoot me, were you? Not over a little intrusion like this."

Morgan sent her a level look meant to convey his resignation, but it came across as the annoyance it truly was.

"Well, I promise this will only take a moment," she said, "then I'll be out of your hair."

Morgan blew out a breath. This woman had made more trouble for him than all of his other clients combined. Her sole priority with him was obvious, climbing higher on her company's stepladder, another way she and Annie differed. Annie had been a dedicated teacher who'd cared whether or not her students grasped the math concepts she'd taught. Her email box had always been full of questions and she'd answered every one. Morgan's back stiffened and the lines of his mouth flattened, reminded of another email of hers.

Morgan opened the folder and sifted through the papers, his mind not focused on the words on the pages, while Lara leaned back into the corner of the couch with her arms raised on the cushions and her legs crossed towards him. When he'd first met her, he could admit he'd been slightly fascinated by the differences he saw in her and Annie. For one thing, Annie kept her short fingernails and toenails natural, unpainted. Lara always had red polish on her long nails and he'd never seen her toes. Lara wore her blond hair in a stiff style, too perfect. Annie's brown waves could at times be unruly like when she woke up in the morning. But those times when the two of them had just woken up, she overwhelmed him, her scent and her softness. He would slide her body beneath his and kiss her until she writhed beneath him. Her scars didn't make her vulnerable; the way she faced him first thing in the morning, soft and rumpled, did. With nothing to hide, the way she walked around the house barefoot, in a tank top, and wearing a pair of his boxer shorts, made him want her all the more. Lara in her red suit and matching high heels made him think she kept a lot of things hidden.

He chuckled to himself now. Annie had been right. Lara did wear power suits and at eight o'clock at night. Didn't this woman own a pair of jeans?

Morgan forced himself to concentrate on the

papers in his lap and began reading.

"The important parts are highlighted," Lara said. "Then where we need your signature is flagged on each page."

"There are about a hundred flags," Morgan said.

Lara grinned and shrugged her bare shoulders. "My boss wants everything just so."

Morgan groaned inwardly as Lara slipped off her high heels, tucking her bare feet beneath her on the couch.

"What are you doing here all by yourself?" she said, looking around the empty living room. "I thought you were a happily married man."

Morgan slanted a dark sideways look at her and didn't answer. After getting about half-way through the tome of papers, he paused. "I can't promise to provide those kinds of numbers for the new slim line airpacks. If you'll agree to half that many, I can fill in as much as possible and hope to reach your number by the end of the year."

"I don't know. Richard specifically came up with that number himself."

"Then I should talk to him directly."

Lara shook her head, all of her blond hair swaying in unison as she did. "He's on vacation this weekend. That's why yours truly is here taking care of business before he gets back."

"Doesn't he carry his cell?"

She scoffed. "Not to the Turks and Caicos."

Morgan raked a hand through his hair.

"I might be able to get him to agree on fewer if we could add an inventory sheet from you," she said. "Do you have anything like that from last year as an indicator?"

"I think I do. But it will be in my truck right now."

"I'll wait." She grinned, gazing up at him beneath long lashes.

Morgan blew out a breath and retrieving his gun once again, walked outside to his truck.

When the door closed behind Morgan, Lara stood, looking around the empty living room. She walked to the front window, watching Morgan rifle through the back of his truck.

She turned at the sound of his cell ringing from its place on the coffee table. Smiling to herself, she answered it.

Morgan stepped through the front door in time to see Lara set his phone down. "What were you doing?"

"Just letting your wife know that you and I were in the middle of a business meeting."

Morgan reddened, his jaw muscles flexing. "You shouldn't have done that."

"She gave me a message to give you. Would you like to know what she said?" Lara grinned. "She sounded very upset."

"I'd like for you to leave. Tell Richard that anything else he wants will have to wait until Monday."

"But I can't get in touch with him until he gets back."

"Text him. I may be just a fireman, but I happen to know the Turks and Caicos has fine cell reception. My next-door neighbor spends every March there. They're down there right now as a matter of fact.

Texted me from there just this morning to ask me to look for a package on their front porch."

Lara's brow creased and she crossed her arms over her chest. "Your wife needs you to come home right away. Your dog is dead."

Without another word, Morgan placed a firm hand on Lara's back and escorted her to the door, closing it harder than necessary behind her. He scooped up the bundle of papers from the couch and tossed them into his gym bag. He turned to his phone, where Lara had left it, to call Annie, but just as his hand closed around it, a text alert chimed.

"All off-duty personnel respond. Fully-involved structure fire at the old textile mill on Goddard Road."

Morgan cursed aloud. *Just my luck.*

Chapter 7

Annie picked herself up off the floor. Despite the protest of her muscles, she could have shriveled up on that tile and disappeared. She dialed the phone in her hand now. The vet's answering machine picked up, giving her the number for after-hour emergencies.

"We'll send someone over to collect Glenda's body. Do you want them to come right away or wait until morning?"

Annie couldn't think straight but her gut told her right away.

Twenty minutes passed, sitting with her back against the wall of the kitchen beside the dog's bed just the way she had the night Glenda had become a mother, when she heard a knock on the front door. Her tired brain hoped Morgan had lost his key. But when Annie opened the door, a man of about twenty stood there dressed in white jeans and polo shirt. A tattoo of a pit bull's face decorated the lower part of his left bicep.

"I'm from Richland Creek Veterinarian Clinic. I'm sorry for your loss."

"She's in the kitchen." Annie's voice cracked on the last word.

She opened the front door to let the young man inside; following him to the kitchen's threshold, where she froze, unable to watch him remove Glenda. From the edge of the room, as close as she could get without looking, she remembered Glenda the way she had been.

Taylor Armstrong left Engine 2 and rushed over to Morgan. "You're the first lieutenant here, sir. Lieutenant Stanton is on his way and my lieutenant is out on family leave."

"What have we got?" Morgan stepped out of his Landcruiser dressed in t-shirt, jeans, and a pair of black steel-toe boots in front of the old textile mill, now a storehouse for various businesses.

"Homeless are known to occupy the inside of the mill."

"Dispatch Ladder Two." Morgan went around back to retrieve his turnout gear.

"Already done, sir. Seven-minute ETA."

"Alright. Good work." Morgan stepped into his turnout pants, pulling the suspenders over his shoulders. "In the meantime, I want all four quadrants covered. Tell the pumper truck to hook up to the hydrant across the street." He shrugged into his turnout jacket.

"Yes, sir." The younger man got on his radio and relayed everything Morgan had just said. "What about a scout, sir?"

"That's me."

"But sir, the assistant chief is en route from home too. He won't be here for at least ten more minutes. You're the highest ranking officer on scene as of now."

"We don't have time to wait."

Taylor hesitated. "Yes, sir."

Morgan kneeled down on the cracked pavement with his back to the younger man who lifted the old airpack onto Morgan's back while Morgan attached the waist strap securing the shoulder harness in place. He stood. "I'll be glad when the department springs for the slim-line models. These are like carrying around a sack of concrete."

"Yes, sir."

"I want a straight line of water through that visible hole in the C Quadrant roof." Morgan pointed to right above the red brick building's main entrance. "What we can't see can hurt us. Then call Parker Fire Department and ask them to stand by for assistance."

"I'm on it." Taylor spoke into the radio as Morgan headed for the entrance to the one-story mill.

"Don't forget this," Eddie Stanton, who'd just arrived with Engine 2, called out to Morgan. He held out Morgan's PASS device to him.

Morgan accepted the safety alarm that would emit a loud, pulsating shriek if he didn't move for longer than thirty seconds, and hooked it to the carabiner on his turnout jacket's waist.

He stepped into the building, thick with black smoke and began silently counting his steps.

"The puppies will need a source of heat now that Glenda is gone." The vet had also said that Annie would have to bottle-feed the puppies herself.

Annie drove in the darkness towards the pet store but at the last minute, detoured to her mother's condominium, parking her truck next to a silver Honda Prelude. She knocked on the door next to her mother's. No one answered. She tried peering through the window, but wood shutters blocked her view.

After knocking again and waiting a few more

moments in silence, she turned the knob. It wasn't something she'd planned; desperation had taken a hold of her. She had to speak to someone about her mother.

To her surprise, the door was unlocked and she pushed it open. The musty smell hit her first. The air-conditioner hadn't been running inside. From the strength of the smell, Sarah Greis must have been gone for quite some time, but she wouldn't, no one in Florida would've, turned off the air conditioning. Too much mildew. The unit, identical to her mother's, opened into the living room. But the velvet blue couch was gone, and the two mismatched club chairs too. No television set. Further in, the old wood kitchen table and chairs weren't there, empty cupboards, not even a magnet on the fridge. Annie turned back. She could see Mrs. Greis' living room as it had been, she'd been over there enough as a girl. Something was very wrong.

A strange sound came to her from the backyard, something like a baby crying, but as she took a step towards the door, the darkness and the silence overwhelmed her, completely alone. She froze, unable to take another step. The last time she'd found herself alone in the dark like this, her ex-boyfriend had attacked her.

The sound of a car pulling into the front of Mrs. Greis' condo filled the air and for a moment, Annie feared it was Mrs. Greis, returning home. Headlights lit up the front room through the windows. Annie ducked, afraid of being seen, her heart racing. She ran that way, with her head down, to the front door, praying that whoever it was wouldn't see her inside this woman's condominium.

The driver got out and walked into the main office, slamming the door behind them.

Annie let out the breath she'd held and promised herself never to do anything like that again. She would find out what she needed to know the legal way from now on, not from breaking and entering.

Inside the pet store, Annie tried to regain her sense of normalcy. She was just like everyone else out at nine o'clock at night, buying dog food. Normal. She passed a pen of puppies rolling and frolicking in cedar shavings and found an entire aisle dedicated to puppies too young to eat solid foods. Standing there looking at the innocent little faces staring back at her from the puppy formula labels, she couldn't hold back the tears that filled her eyes. The puppies' loss, like hers, hit too close to the bone.

But I'm not a child anymore. I can take care of myself.

She placed the items from her cart on the conveyer belt, a heat lamp for day, a heating blanket for night, tiny bottles for hand-feeding, and cans of powdered puppy formula.

"Since we don't know exactly when Glenda passed over," the vet had said over the phone, "the puppies are likely going to be pretty hungry. Try to feed them every two to three hours. If they fall asleep while nursing, they've had enough. Call me if you have any questions."

"Annie Morgan?"

Annie looked up, suddenly dragged out of her thoughts. "Yes," she said to the woman behind the register.

"I'm Betty Vitkevich. I was a friend of your mother's."

The stark contrast between Nancy Carlucci and Betty Vitkevich hit Annie as she looked at the older woman. She wore her hair in a black pixie cut, her nails were short and unpainted, with no rings on her fingers. "Oh, yes, Mrs. Vitkevich. I've wanted to talk to you about my mother."

The woman's posture stiffened.

"To thank you. I know you were with her when it happened."

"Yes. I was so sorry about it all. I would've called you, but I didn't know what to say. Your mother was a dear woman."

"Thank you." Annie pulled three twenties from her wallet. "Do you know how I can reach Sarah Greis? I wanted to speak to all of my mother's friends."

"She's been up in Michigan visiting her son for the past month. She probably won't be back until Memorial Day."

"What about Tabbie Weaver?"

Betty Vitkevich chuckled. "Tabbie never goes anywhere. Can't afford to. She's on a fixed income. And since she broke her nose, she hasn't been out of her condo. Won't even answer the door."

Mrs. Vitkevich took Annie's money then hesitated.

"Is there something wrong?" Annie said.

The woman seemed to change her mind about whatever it was she wanted to say. "You have a puppy at home?" she said as she put Annie's new purchases into plastic bags.

Annie smiled. "Five to be exact."

"I had a dog. Ran off two weeks ago today. Haven't seen her since."

"Her?"

"Yes," Mrs. Vitkevich counted out Annie's change, "she was an old sheep dog mix with a blond coat."

It couldn't be.

"Sweetest dog. I found her in the trash when she was just a puppy. Tried to hide her from that man, the condo president. But as soon as he suspected me, he wouldn't leave me alone. Hounding me day and night until finally, he caught me taking her for a walk. He kicked me out right then and there. I didn't have a choice, had to move in with my daughter. But the yard wasn't fenced. So she always got out. Then one day, she didn't come back."

Annie couldn't ask if the dog's name was Glenda because then she'd have to tell her that her dog was dead. "What were you doing at my mother's the night she died?"

"I stopped by after work. She was paying me for her part of the lottery tickets."

"Did she write you a check?"

"Yes," Betty Vitkevich smiled, "she always did. How did you know?"

"Oh, just a hunch."

As a kid Morgan had been fascinated with Darth Vader, not so much with his plan to take over the galaxy but with his mask, the cool sound it made when Darth Vader breathed in and out. The first time Morgan had suited up with an airpack, he'd felt just like his dark hero. Now, he counted his audible breaths inside his own mask, a trick he'd picked up from one of his instructors at Lively Vocational Technical School in Tallahassee back when he'd been just a student.

"Counting your breaths can be a meditation, keeping your mind focused on the task at hand," he'd said.

Morgan had never forgotten it and had used it every time he went inside a structure fire.

He had reached the middle of the building, counting his steps as he went. On hands and knees now, he swept the floor with his hands outstretched in front of him, searching for victims, counting his breaths. Nicky, directly behind him, crawled along on his hands and knees, holding onto Morgan's pant leg to keep them from getting separated.

Blackness surrounded Morgan. The gray smoke swirled over his head. Water from the hoses outside hissed and evaporated all around him. The cavernous space, mostly empty now except for some metal sheeting, had housed textile equipment, sold off shortly after the mill shut its doors. As his thoughts drifted, Annie's beautiful face popped into his mind. He tried to push her away, but he couldn't let her image go. Here he risked his life for people he didn't know and there a woman sitting at home who needed him just as much if not more. He'd hurt her so many times in the past, unintentionally of course, but he'd reached his limit. He couldn't look into her eyes and see the hurt and disappointment anymore. He couldn't remember the last time he'd looked into her eyes sober without feeling his gut clench.

Morgan's hand bumped into something hard. His heart beat sped as he prayed it wasn't a body. He looked through the lens of the infrared camera. Just an old pallet lay there, probably a bed for one of the people who made the place their home. But not two feet ahead, there was a body. As he inched closer, he could see through the heat-seeking camera that it was a woman's body with no indication of life.

The fire contained itself to the roof at the moment. How it had started would be up to FDLE's experts to decide. But this discovery took the whole situation and turned it on its head. Now this was a potential murder scene.

He pressed the button on his radio. "I've got a victim here. No pulse. Victim may have been living inside. Send me a RIT team for removal. I'm on the D side of the building."

"Okay copy," Eddie replied from the outside, "D side of the building. RIT team is making entry."

Taking several more sweeping scans over the space with his camera as he waited for help, he was satisfied that any other occupants had already fled.

"Command, Engine Two crew has completed the searched of the building," he said into his radio. "We'll be exiting the building."

Light from the trucks hit his eyes and he blinked, adjusting from the dark. The RIT team carried the woman outside. She was probably in her sixties, dressed in a rag, and with no identification on her whatsoever.

The next morning dawned too soon for Annie's eyes. The light breaking through the wood shutters covering her bedroom windows caused her to close them and turn away.

She'd brought the puppies and their bed upstairs into her room last night. The closest thing they had to a mother now, she would have to keep them close. She looked at the brass clock on her bedside table.

Seven o'clock.

Only three hours ago, she'd been on the floor with them, holding two bottles in each hand. That procedure left one puppy out, always the same one, the runt, Glenda's lookalike. Smaller than the rest of the litter and slower, she couldn't compete. So Annie had come up with a creative solution. Sitting cross-legged, she'd laid the puppy on her own thigh and rested the bottle on her calf. Within minutes, little Glenda had fallen fast asleep.

Annie dressed then refilled the bottles with warm water and puppy formula. As she did, something her mother had knitted years before popped into her mind. The silliest thing Annie had ever seen then, meant to be an organizer for the arm rest on her couch, it hadn't been quite right and kept slipping off. It had little pockets for holding the remote, her reading glasses, a twelve-ounce bottle of Pepsi, and a rolled up TV Guide.

Annie knew how she would put it to use.

After the puppies had their breakfast and she had eaten a cup of yogurt, she got into her Landcruiser. On the threshold of her mother's condo, she fished around inside her purse for the key. When she couldn't find it, she reluctantly knocked on the condo president's office door. She would have to admit she'd lost the key he'd entrusted her with.

Once again, he answered the door with a napkin under his chin. The room smelled of pastries and he carried with him the strong scent of coffee as he led the way to her mother's door.

After he'd unlocked the condo, he turned to her, the smell of his morning coffee emanating from him. "I trust you will be able to locate that key by the end of the month when your mother's condo goes on the market."

She nodded and went inside to get away from the unbearable heat and from the little man who might very well be responsible for her mother's death.

Morgan had been there. On the floor, sat his duffel bag with all of his clothes inside.

Her eyes widened as she took in the now empty living room. It had been wiped clean, not a knick-knack or book in sight. She walked into her mother's bedroom and released the breath she held. While he had packed up her mother's odds and ends, he hadn't touched her bedroom. Everything remained the same. The clothes inside her closet and the clothes inside her dresser were still there. She didn't have a lot of time to be angry; she had to get back to the puppies.

Annie first opened the top drawer to her mother's dresser and gasped.

She had a gun?

Annie picked it up, feeling its heavy weight in her hand.

Why? Had it been because she found herself alone at night? Or had there been a more pressing reason, like someone who'd threatened her?

She slid the gun into her own purse and opened the closet. Above her head on the shelf were boxes of shoes reaching all the way to the ceiling. Below the clothes were plastic bins with see-through drawers. Annie pulled open the one with knitted fabric inside. It wasn't a question of *if* her mother had kept it, it was just a matter of finding *where*. She dug through handmade scarfs, mittens, and hats, things her mother might have worn only once. And there it sat, the navy blue knitted organizer that had never been.

As she drove home, thinking of a thousand ways to dismember a six-foot fireman, she swerved to miss a squirrel that darted out in front of her. The things in the back of the truck shifted.

My mother!

The last thing she'd put back there had been her mother's ashes. She slammed on the brakes now, realizing too late her urn hadn't been inside the condo where she'd left it. The book shelves had been cleared. She hadn't seen that brass sailing cup anywhere. She burst into tears as she yanked the wheel, turning back to the complex.

Inside, she frantically searched the living room, running into the bedroom, the closet, the bathroom, but to her horror, she didn't see the cup anywhere. She dug her phone from her purse, bursting from the condo, pressing the number for Morgan.

She squeezed the truck's steering wheel in a white-knuckled grip with one hand and the phone with the other. She had been angry when he'd donated her mother's things without her knowing, but this didn't enter into the realms of comparison.

Of course, he didn't answer. So she left a delirious voice message explaining in a hysterical tantrum-voice that he'd thrown out her mother!

Monday morning, Morgan awoke at the fire station, groggy from lack of sleep the night before. The closed blinds blocked the sunlight, keeping the room from getting too hot. He only slept past seven a.m. at the station on mornings after calls like the one they'd had last night.

He sat up. He'd heard his phone ringing though he hadn't been fully awake. He checked the missed calls now and put the phone back down on the bedside table that separated his bed from the empty one beside it. He refused to talk to her.

Eddie popped his head into Morgan's darkened bunkroom. "Was that Annie?"

Morgan rolled onto his side and raked a hand over his hair crumpled from sleep. "Yeah," his voice thick and groggy.

"You'd better take care of her, Morgan," Eddie said in a voice much too alert so early in the morning, "or you're gonna lose her."

"She doesn't need me anymore. She's got that physicist, her best friend. Maybe he can give her what she wants." Morgan blew out a long breath. "And what do you know about it? Mind your own damn business."

"Fool! My friend, you are my business. That Lara woman is in love with you, and don't think for a second that Annie isn't smart enough to already know that. She teaches Math to college students for Christ's sake. She's smarter than you and me put together. So what is she doing with you anyway? Ever asked yourself that question before? Because if you haven't, now would be a good time to start."

"This from a man on his second marriage."

"How do you think I got so smart?"

Morgan shot him a dark look meant to get rid of him, but it didn't work. Eddie walked into the room and sat on the empty bunk opposite Morgan.

"Don't make the same mistake I made."

"You lost Becky to another man?"

Eddie nodded. "I thought if I played it cool, let everything blow over, in time she'd realize that things between us weren't so bad. You want to know what she was doing while I was playing it cool? Filing for divorce, that's what."

Morgan placed an elbow on either knee and let his head fall into his hands. "Is she still married to her dentist?"

"Married him the same day the divorce was final."

Morgan picked up his phone and stared at the black screen.

"Now you're using your smarts." With that Eddie slapped his knee, causing Morgan to flinch, and got up. "And get your lazy ass out of bed," he said from the doorway. "Breakfast will be ready in five minutes."

"Annie."

No answer came.

He dropped the spare key back under the fake rock in the azaleas and stepped into Annie's nice, neat, comfortable home where he'd spent a thousand quiet evenings. He admired the antique scarred wood table in the center of the living room, the brightly lit corner where she kept a Ficus tree, the red, white, and blue throw pillows atop the white fabric sofa, all his doing. The lack of clutter, shelves full of books, and expensive vase, all him, making it a place for adults, not children or dogs. She wasn't thinking straight.

He hadn't told Annie he'd returned home from Italy. He'd driven straight from the airport and had the taxi drop him off. With Morgan out of the picture now, he would surprise his future wife. He would relish her expression when she saw him there, surprise or anger, it didn't matter.

Instead of coming back later and calling her phone as he should've done in the first place, he went further inside their house, making himself at home. Every time Annie had been unattached in the past, he'd been in a relationship and vice versa. His opportunity had finally arrived after almost two decades. Research trip be damned.

He passed the kitchen and frowned when he saw the litter of puppies sleeping there. They would have to go. This wasn't a kennel.

He took the creaky steps one at a time. At the top, the nursery that sat unused, the one with the elephant wallpaper, didn't look right. Annie had changed it. A part of him had wished that she wouldn't have a baby. Children only complicate things, or they had for his father, and then they end up with everything when you're dead. Having children had meant nothing more to his father than another mouth to feed. All he'd ever cared for had been his precious antique Mercedes convertible that he'd kept covered in the garage. And for as long as he'd lived, his son had never laid a hand on it.

Whose car is it now, Dad?

He stepped inside the room to find it full of Annie's office things, her framed wedding picture, which he placed face-down on the desk now, her files, and her books. She thought she would simply quit her job and cut him out of her life?

A poster hung on the wall full of her neat handwriting, names he didn't recognize. But one he did. His.

Suspects? What the hell was she doing?

He laughed aloud. She was playing detective now.

He drifted out of her new office with a smile on his face. The last time he'd been inside her bedroom, it had been to help her bring home an armoire to house the television and DVR. At the doorway, he paused, imagining her lying in her bed dressed in a silk nightdress, her brown hair spilling over her pillow, her perfect mouth smiling up at him. Keeping his hands from her body, her small waist and turgid breasts all these years attested to his superior intellect. Only a man with incredible power over his animal brain could accomplish such a feat, especially considering the amount of time they'd spent together over the years, time her husband had been away.

He'd always suspected that Morgan had only married her for a trophy, something else he could pin to his chest like his badge. He'd never really appreciated her mind. His ego couldn't handle a woman with a brain like hers.

Bryant set his suitcase down on top of the steamer trunk at the foot of the bed and went to her dresser. He opened the top drawer and found it, the lace and silk teddy she'd answered the door in last

Christmas. Bryant could still see Annie in it and had to stop himself thinking about it now and concentrate on unpacking. He slipped the teddy into the outer pouch of his suitcase.

If he unpacked his clothes now, he might seem too presumptuous. Instead, he went downstairs to the kitchen to prepare their lunch. They would eat together as they'd done every day since middle school.

His insides quivered for a cigarette, something he'd given up to please Annie. She wanted him to live long enough to sail around the world, his dream after he retired. Now they could make the trip together. Things were finally going his way.

Morgan picked up his phone to dial Annie's number when he saw that he had a voice message waiting from her. He pulled a white t-shirt over his head and listened. He froze when he heard what she said.

He'd lost her mother? What did that mean?

He had a million things he needed to do that morning, at the top of the list, deal with Lara's boss, Richard. But that got moved to the bottom now along with every other call he had to make. He stripped his bunk, threw the sheets in his locker (he'd wash them next shift), stepped into his boots and laced them while trying to decipher the rest of her message. She yelled through most of it, causing it to break up. So he'd only caught bits and pieces. But he got the gist. He'd messed up.

Anger had to be a good sign though. She hadn't given up on him yet.

On the drive home from her mother's condo, Annie glanced down at the knitted cozy. It would finally be useful. She decided she'd have to put off her trip to Goodwill to ask about her mother's ashes until after she'd fed the puppies; they came first. But she pressed the accelerator a little harder anyway.

What if her mother got sold for two dollars and put on some stranger's mantle? She could never forgive Morgan if that happened.

She opened her front door and the scent of grilled cheese frying in the kitchen hit her. Morgan had come home. Suddenly all of her anger at him melted away. They would go to Goodwill together and get her mother back. All would be well.

"When you didn't hear back from me, you probably thought I disappeared."

The voice was wrong.

Annie froze in the foyer, keys in hand, mouth open. Her tired brain took a few moments to comprehend. Instead of her husband making the two of them lunch, Bryant inexplicably stood inside her house instead of halfway around the world.

"I just needed some time to let the news that you'd quit your job settle in. I couldn't imagine going into work and not seeing you anymore."

She staggered into the kitchen. "Bryant, what are you doing here?"

"Making lunch. I admit that I was angry when I first read your email."

"You came all the way home to tell me this?" she said, interrupting.

"No, of course not." He chuckled and tilted his

head, looking at her as though she were a child. "I came home to tell you that don't owe me any explanation."

"That wasn't necessary." Her tone was hard but he didn't seem to notice.

"And with Morgan gone, I've got the opportunity to say this to you in person now."

"Before you say anything, maybe we should talk."

He shook his head. "There's nothing to say but this," he stepped toward her with outstretched arms, "I love you, Annie. I've always loved you."

"Bryant," she hesitated, folding her arms over her waist.

His brow creased. She recalled the last time she'd told a man she didn't love him. She'd ended up in the ER. But the thought of sending him away and being alone now sent chills up and down her spine. She didn't have to be in love with Bryant.

Do I have to break his heart?

"Bryant, there's no easy way to say this to you. You know that I love you."

His eyes softened again as he gazed at her.

"But I don't love you the way I love Morgan."

"Morgan." Bryant scoffed and turned back to the stove. "How can you love him, Annie? I've never understood how you and I could have the kind of connection we have, the kind that most people would kill for, and you go and marry him."

"Bryant, you understand. I know you do. You loved Candace the same way I love Morgan."

"No, Annie. I loved Candace because she loved me. I couldn't help myself. She had a way of admiring me that I couldn't resist. But then I realized how inane it was. We had nothing in common, and I couldn't live with someone who put me on a pedestal. It was sad really, the way she made a fool of herself."

"I know you don't mean that. I know you were hurt by her. You deserved better than being cheated on."

Bryant's cheeks reddened. She had said too much. "I'm sorry. I shouldn't have brought her up. Let's talk about something else. I need to feed the puppies."

Bryant flipped their grilled cheese sandwiches while Annie unpacked the knitted bottle cozy she'd brought home from her mother's. Her mother. She had to get rid of Bryant before it was too late to rescue her mother's ashes.

"Tell me about your trip," she said casually while she filled five bottles with warm water and puppy formula.

Bryant chatted about his week in Italy, his work and his coworkers. Annie sat down cross-legged on the tile floor in front of the puppies' bed, listening. She placed four bottles in the cozy and situated Blue, Benji, Petey, and Tabitha in a line in front of it, one at each nipple. Then she scooped up little Glenda and placed her in her lap, holding her bottle for her while she fed. Her limp little body, unlike her brothers and sisters, didn't search for milk with hungry eyes, didn't seem eager to feed at all. After all she'd been through, losing her mother, she must be exhausted.

When the puppies had drunk their fill, she placed each of them back in their bed and joined Bryant at the table. He'd filled two glasses with iced tea and cut their sandwiches diagonally down the middle. "Thank you. You didn't have to fix lunch. I'm really not hungry."

"You need to eat, Annie." He looked into her eyes in that way he had. "You need someone to look after you, not someone who's at work all the time. You and I have spent more time together since you married Morgan than we ever did before." Bryant laughed.

"He has his business."

Bryant held up a hand. "I've heard them all. Remember who you're talking to."

"I do remember who I'm talking to, the man who's been my friend for a long, long time."

"And confidante, and shopping buddy, and theater companion, and dinner date, and..."

"I know, Bryant. You're right. You have been there for me, and for that, I will always owe you."

"You don't owe me anything. It's my pleasure." He held up his tea glass. "I want to do this for you for the rest of our lives."

Annie shook her head. "I can't do that to Morgan. He means too much to me. My marriage means too much to me. I have to at least try."

"What do call what you've been doing for seven long years?" Bryant's fist came down hard on the table, sloshing tea from Annie's glass and rattling their plates. His mouth turned down into a flat line but he remained silent, looking at his fist.

Annie got up for a towel to clean up the spilled tea, but his hand snaked out and wrapped around her wrist. "Annie, don't do this to me."

"I'm sorry."

He dropped his hand. "You're going to regret this one day."

"I already do. I don't want to lose you, but I can see now that there's nothing else I can do."

"Then don't."

"I don't have a choice. I'm married to Morgan."

Bryant sighed. "Then he's the luckiest man on Earth, to have the loyalty of such a woman."

Annie shook her head.

"You just don't see yourself the way I do." Bryant stood, taking both of Annie's hands in his and pulling her to him.

This was it. In all the years she'd known him, he had never embraced her, hardly ever even touched her except the occasional brush of his arm past hers as they'd walked down the city sidewalk in search of the next antique. This was truly goodbye. He hugged her tight.

Panic seized her abdomen. As soon as he walked out that door, she would truly be alone. No more Saturdays at flea markets together, no more Friday nights at the movies, no more Sundays on his boat. She clung to him. She didn't know if she could go through with goodbye. She couldn't count on Morgan to be there for her whenever she needed him. Bryant had. He'd given her friendship. Bryant had helped her make her home into what it was. And she couldn't, absolutely could not, face being alone there.

Then the front door of her beloved beach cottage opened. Without a glance in that direction Annie's exhausted mind knew that Morgan had walked through the door and a whole lot of trouble headed her way.

Chapter 8

Morgan took one look at the two of them, Bryant and Annie holding each other in his own kitchen, and cursed.

If he was any other man he would've run upstairs for the shot gun he kept under his side of the bed and run him off, or he would've burst into the kitchen and punched Bryant in his smug, uptight, condescending face, but Morgan was not any other man. He didn't need to prove anything to Bryant or to Annie or to himself. Bryant was scared of him; Morgan had seen it that night he'd surprised Bryant on the driveway. Bryant had jumped into his car and locked the doors as soon as he'd set eyes on him. Morgan was man enough to defend what was his. He just didn't know anymore if he still wanted what was his.

He turned on his heel and walked back out the door.

"Morgan!" Annie's voice was high, strained.

Good. He'd kept his mouth shut once too often about Bryant. If she wanted that man, she could damn well have him.

He was already inside his truck, starting the engine when Annie reached the driver's door.

"Morgan, it's not what you think," she said through the glass.

A stony expression met her. "Tell me what I think."

"Bryant is going back to Italy for the rest of the

year."

Morgan rolled down the window. "Tell him to send me a postcard," he said. "On second thought, he's got your email address."

Annie looked away quickly at the sight of his scowl. "Morgan, what you read came as just as big a shock to me."

"I don't see how that's possible. The two of you are connected at the hip. And once again as soon as my back is turned, he slithers in."

"That's not true."

Morgan shot her a level look.

"And what about Lara? You've seen her behind my back."

Morgan's brow furrowed. "That's business, Annie, and you know it."

"You've had private dinners with her I didn't know about."

"Business dinners."

"Then why wasn't your wife invited? You can't deny there's something between you two. I saw the way she looked at you."

"The only thing between us is business, Annie." He stared into her eyes, daring her to argue. When she didn't, he said, "I came home because you left a message I didn't understand. I wanted to clear things up between us, and instead, I find you in Bryant's arms."

All of her anger at him returned full force and she boldly met his eyes. "How dare you give my mother away to Goodwill!"

"Care to explain that?"

"You cleaned out her condo?"

Morgan nodded.

Annie folded her arms under her breasts. "Well, there was a brass urn that looked like a sailing cup. You took it!"

Morgan continued to stare at her, his jaw clenched.

"It had my mother's ashes in it. How could you? You gave her away!"

"I'll take care of it, Annie."

She closed her mouth. She had expected him to argue.

"I'll drive there now and fix it. I'll bet they haven't even unloaded the boxes I dropped off."

"And who said it was okay to give all of her stuff away?"

"You have so much on your mind right now, I figured while I was there, I'd take something off your to-do list."

Annie scowled at him but unfolded her arms. "Don't even so much as touch any more of her things."

Her voice had been a warning and his rose to match it. "All right."

"I'll go through her room. There are some more things I want to keep."

Morgan cleared his throat and stared at the front of the cottage, Bryant still inside. "What happened with the dog?" he said, his voice calmer. "I got your message that she died. Where is she?"

Annie looked down at the shells beneath her leather sandals. Her face reddened. The sound of Lara's voice answering his phone still echoed through her mind. An angry tear slipped down her cheek.

"The vet came for her."

"I'm sorry I wasn't here, Ann."

Morgan hadn't called her by that name in a long time. "Do you mean that? You're really sorry you weren't here?"

"You know I do." His voice felt like a caress. "I would've come home and taken care of her for you."

"But you didn't." The accusation in her voice was clear. "Was Miss Powersuit at my mother's condo?"

Morgan blew out a breath. "It's a long story."

"I've got time." She tapped her foot on the driveway causing the seashells packed beneath her foot to rattle.

"The department had a training exercise at Station Four the other day. We used location tracking on our phones to locate each other without using visuals. Your phone has the app too; I installed it. When we finished, I forgot to turn mine off. She found me there."

"Did she stay all night?"

Morgan's head whipped towards Annie. "What kind of a question is that?"

"One I want an answer to."

"No!" Morgan scowled. "No, she did not stay all night or even half an hour. She left as soon as I told her to."

Annie closed her mouth on her next question. He'd told her to leave. "Then why didn't you come home?"

"I couldn't. There was a fire."

More of the heat left her voice. "Was anyone hurt?"

"Nope."

"Well, I'm glad you're safe."

"Annie, look, can we start over here?"

"I'd like to."

At that moment, Bryant chose to walk out of the house, and Morgan's expression turned to stone once more. He got out of his truck.

"I've called a cab," Bryant said from a safe distance on the front porch. "Should be here any second." An unmarked navy blue sedan pulled into the driveway behind Morgan's Landcruiser. "And there it is."

Annie looked from one man to the other, afraid of what Morgan would say to her old friend.

Bryant stepped up and extended a hand to Morgan. "Take care of her."

Morgan looked down at it for a moment. "I always have."

Annie's eyes pleaded with him to be civil.

Morgan shook the man's hand, his jaw muscles flexing.

Bryant turned to Annie. "He's a lucky man."

"And he knows it." Morgan's drawl held a note of threat.

She smiled up at Bryant. "Thanks. Bryant, where will you go?"

"Back to work, in Italy." Bryant walked past her and got into his cab, luggage in hand.

She watched him leave. The finality of it surprised her, the last time she would see him. She wrapped her arms around herself.

Turning back to Morgan, who lifted his brow, she shrugged. "He was here when I got home."

"Get in," Morgan grunted.

Annie ran back inside for her purse. She peeked into the kitchen on the still sleeping puppies. But Little Glenda did not sleep; she whimpered. Annie couldn't just leave her there suffering. She scooped up the tiny bundle and wrapped her body in a clean kitchen towel. "You're coming with me."

Annie told Morgan all about the puppy and how worried she was. Little Glenda needed to be checked out by the vet as soon as possible, yet desperation drove Annie to pick up her mother's urn first for fear it would be lost forever. Morgan made up her mind for her when he pulled into the Goodwill parking lot next to a familiar silver Honda Prelude, the same one she'd seen parked near her mother's condo.

"This won't take a minute," Morgan said. "Then we'll take her to the vet and get her checked out."

The man that greeted Morgan at the drop-off looked like he'd be more at home as a maître d than working in the dusty back room of a donation center. Over his thin frame he wore loose-fitting dress pants and a jacket draped over his narrow shoulders. As he listened to her husband explain the situation, Annie noticed that he stood about a foot shorter than Morgan. As she looked around, she saw that the same car she'd seen parked in front of Tabbie Weaver's condo was parked in an employee's parking spot. She got out too.

"This isn't actually the first one of these we've received," the man was saying to Morgan, one hand on his hip, the other in the air. "Sometimes, in their grief, people accidentally pack away Mom or Dad or Great Aunt Wilma along with all of their belongings.

Then, in a positive fit, they call us, asking if we've already sold their dearly departed family member. It usually works out alright though."

The man pointed to a shelf behind a row of boxes in the massive warehouse as the three of them walked inside together. "This is where we keep things that we think might be missed. We've found engagement rings inside their original boxes. Brand new toys still in their boxes aren't uncommon around Christmas time. Once we even unwrapped a kitten the day after Christmas. It turned out fine; the little girl came back with her daddy and all was well."

Morgan followed the man wearing a pair of Bruno Maglis that slipped on his feet as he walked and guessed that employees must have first pick of donations. Not a bad deal.

"We only hold onto things that we feel weren't meant to be donated for about a week. Sometimes people come back for them. Sometimes they don't. As you can see, yours isn't the only urn we've got with us today."

Annie nudged Morgan. "That's it," she said, pointing up.

On the floor of the warehouse there must have been at least a half dozen sofas. One blue velvet camel back in particular caught her eye—Sarah Greis' couch. That was it. And there was her kitchen table and chairs.

The man picked up a ladder, but Morgan waved him away. "This is it." Morgan reached to the third shelf where her mother's urn sat, safe and sound.

"Ah, the sailing cup. We wondered about that one. It's obviously an urn, because of the rattling, but none of us could figure out the significance. Was your mother-in-law a sailor?"

"No."

The man looked to Annie for further explanation, but she was too busy looking around the warehouse to realize he'd spoken.

"You can't imagine how upset I was when I discovered my mother's ashes missing. Thank you, Tab," Annie read his name tag, "for holding onto this for us. Is that a family name?"

Tab beamed. "My mother's. Her name's Tabbie."

"Tabbie," Annie said. "My mother had a friend at Sunny Pines named Tabbie."

"My mother's at Sunny Pines."

"Is that right?" Morgan said. "Small world."

"I'm Annie Morgan, nice to meet you, Tab. This is my husband, Chance Morgan. My mother's name was Stella Ann Peters."

The man looked thoughtful. "I've heard mother mention that name. Stella cut her hair."

"Yes, my mother was a beautician. Worked at The Solar Day Spa just down the road."

Tab nodded. "I've dropped mother off there more times than I can count. I sometimes even went in."

"Then you must know some of your mother's other friends, Betty Vitkevich, Nancy Carlucci, Sarah Greis."

"Yes, those names ring a bell, but mother isn't the type to gossip."

"How is she? I heard she broke her nose."

Tab Weaver paused, clearing his throat. "Yes, she was playing with the grandkids when it happened. She's doing much better now. I'll tell her you asked about her."

Annie smiled a smile that didn't reach her eyes; something was wrong here. "Please do that."

Morgan handed Annie the sailing cup urn. She held the puppy in one hand and the urn in the other. "Why *would* your mother choose that shape?"

"I've no idea." She absently rubbed the base of the cup with the pad of her thumb. She yawned, unable to think straight.

"Talk to me."

Annie sighed. "Oh, it's Sarah Greis."

Morgan's lips flattened. "What about her?"

"I don't know. Something's wrong. All of her things were back there inside that Goodwill and she's supposed to be visiting her son."

"Annie, there's something you ought to know. In that mill fire, I was doing a sweep and found a woman's body." He paused. "Turns out it was a woman by that name."

Annie gaped at Morgan. "My mother's neighbor?"

He nodded.

"Betty said she was in Michigan this last month," she whispered, holding tightly to her mother's urn with one hand and Glenda in the crook of her other arm. Annie had reached her limit for losing relationships, and if Glenda didn't make it, she might not either.

"The coroner said she'd been dead for a while. About a month. I needed the information for my report. He also said he'd had to use dental records to identify her because she didn't fit the description of any missing persons and she'd had no ID on her. When I found her, she was dressed in rags. That doesn't sound like something one of your mother's friends would ever do."

"Where's the report now?"

"In my gym bag in the back seat, why?"

"I need to see it." Annie put the urn between her feet on the floor board and pulled out her cell phone. From Morgan's duffel bag, the report he'd been working on, she found the name of Sarah Greis' next of kin, her son.

"Hello, Benjamin Greis," she said into her phone. "This is Annie Morgan. I live in St. Michaels, Florida. We've never met, but our mothers were neighbors. Stella Ann Peters."

"Oh, yes, you're married to the firefighter I spoke to on the phone yesterday. He told me about you and your mother."

"I just wanted to call to say how sorry I am for your loss."

"Thank you, Ms. Morgan. My mother always had nothing but good things to say about Stella. I was sorry to hear of her passing too."

"Thank you."

"How did it happen?"

"Heart attack." Supposedly.

Benjamin Greis was silent. "I'm sorry."

"Thank you. Benjamin, I know this is a terrible time for you and I hope you don't mind my saying this, but since you already know that my husband found your mother, then you know about the way she was dressed when she was found."

"Yes, and the more I've thought about it, the

more confusing it is. No one would've wanted to hurt my mother. Not to mention she would never have been caught in clothes like your husband described. She wasn't a proud woman, but she wouldn't leave the house without getting dressed up first. And she never would've gone anywhere without her purse. I'm sure that she had no business in that mill, and that whoever took her there, killed her. It's as simple as that."

Annie hung up, her mind having reached its limit. If she hadn't been sitting in Morgan's truck, she would've fallen. If there had ever been a doubt before that her mother's death was suspicious, then she knew for sure now. She gazed out the window as they passed a marina surrounded by palm trees. A sudden memory hit her. "She met my father on a sailing boat," she said. "It was the only thing she ever told me about him." Annie looked down at the urn. In her frazzled state, she hadn't bothered to read what had been inscribed until that moment. "Time together passes too quickly."

"She spent most of her life alone, didn't she?" Morgan said.

"Not really. She always had her friends. But in a way, yes. After I moved out, she lived alone. Before I was born, she had her mother and her sisters. Her mother was a widow and worked as a nurse to support them. Both of her sisters married right after high school, married soldiers, then all went their separate ways. Her mother died young. So that left my mother here, alone. She never knew her father either; we had that in common."

"And that's how they met then, on a sailboat?"

"Yes, she told me that it was his father's boat. He

was an excellent sailor. And she fell in love with him that day. That's all she ever said."

"So, you didn't know that your father died overseas, defending the country?"

"No." Annie's head whipped towards Morgan. Eyes wide, she stared at him. "How do you know that?"

"After we take Glenda to the vet, I'll take you back to your mother's and show you. I hope you understand, Annie, I just couldn't keep it from you any longer."

Annie could scarcely breathe. Her father had been a soldier? And he was dead too? She'd never felt so alone as she did in that moment, like the little girl she'd once been instead of thirty years old. Her father, the father she'd never even met, would never have the chance to meet, had just walked out on her forever.

By the time they pulled into the parking lot of the vet's office, some of her initial shock had worn off but she hadn't said a word since Morgan had told her about her father, the man she would never set eyes on.

The puppy hadn't stirred during the ride to the vet's office. The receptionist checked them in and once she saw Glenda, reached across the counter for her. "I'll take her right back."

Annie's heart rate multiplied. "Why'd she do that?"

Morgan put his arm around her. "It's okay. They'll take good care of her."

"Do you think it's just protocol for new puppies? Maybe their immune systems are better off away from the other dogs in the waiting room."

Morgan's eyes softened as he gazed down at Annie's pinched expression. "All we can do right now is wait." He guided her to a chair and sat beside her.

Annie looked down at her empty hands that had held Glenda's puppy. Others like them were there waiting for the back room's door to open and to be chosen. A cream colored Labrador with a liver nose sat beside a young woman with long brown hair. She'd heard that most people resemble their pets, but clearly they didn't. There must be more to it than physical resemblance that brought humans together with their animals. Even though Glenda had belonged to someone else, she'd shown up at Annie's back door, given birth to her puppies in Annie's kitchen, and trusted Annie enough to leave them in her care. Yes, there had to be much, much more to it than physical resemblance.

Annie looked at Morgan sitting next to her, so masculine, so male. He took up so much space just sitting. She looked down at her own lap. Her hands, resting on her thighs, were clasped so tight that her knuckles were white. She held her back straight as a board. Morgan on the other hand leaned back, flipping through the pages of a fishing magazine, with his broad back resting against the back of the chair. His knees spread wide, one of them touched Annie's thigh. Despite their differences, she took comfort in them, in him. She needed him to balance her when she became too rigid, too uptight, and he needed her to remind him that life needed some steadiness, someone to come home to. Morgan was all she had. She was all he had.

The door to the back room opened. All chatter in

the waiting room ceased as they held their collective breaths. Instead of being called back, an assistant came out to Annie. The young woman had brown hair with golden highlights, and her tan skin contrasted with the fuchsia of her scrubs. She squatted in front of Annie, revealing a tattoo on her inner arm that read, "just breathe".

"We're giving her fluids right now. She's a little dehydrated."

Annie leaned forward in her vinyl chair. "Can I sit with her?"

The technician shook her head slightly. "The vet would like me to talk to you about options."

Annie's stomach dropped. She didn't want to lose Glenda's baby. Morgan took her hand in his and squeezed. She'd just lost the first dog she'd ever considered her own even if it wasn't, and now she would lose her namesake.

"First, we can keep Glenda here and feed her," the woman spoke in a hushed tone. "She'll have round the clock care. One of our techs is always here."

Annie didn't like the sound of that, Glenda being separated from her brothers and sister, her home.

"Or we can send you home with a surrogate."

"What do you mean?"

The assistant took a breath. "A stray was brought in yesterday morning. She's obviously a recent mother. We can send her home with you and see if she will feed the puppies for you."

Annie's eyes rounded, and she looked to Morgan who nodded slightly.

"That would make things a whole lot easier on you, Annie."

"Won't her family be looking for her?"

The assistant paused and lowered her voice to barely above a whisper. "Most times in cases like this, no. The mother either wasn't wanted or needed any longer. But she's the sweetest thing. She weighs about fifty pounds and her hair is light like Glenda's."

Annie's heart broke for the unwanted dog she had not even met yet. She bowed her head then nodded. "Okay. Let's do that then. She can come home with us."

The assistant smiled. "Great! I'll go tell the doctor." She went back into the inner sanctum and the door swung closed behind her. As everyone in the waiting room exhaled, chatter began again.

A great weight had been lifted from Annie's shoulders as Morgan pulled her close so that her head rested on his shoulder. "Everything's going to be okay, Ann."

She looked up into his eyes, asking without words if that would be true of the two of them. Would they survive the damage they'd done to their marriage?

Morgan kissed her forehead then leaned his forehead against hers.

The swinging door opened again and a smiling, light haired dog emerged on the end of a pink leash. As if the dog had read the mind of the veterinarian and already knew who would take her home, their gazes locked. They did not separate until the dog closed her eyes as Annie's hand reached out to stroke her head. When the dog opened them again, she gazed back up into Annie's eyes. The dog had one blue eye and one brown eye. Then clear as day, Annie heard the dog say "family". Her hand paused in mid-air. Annie looked to Morgan to see if he had heard the word as well, but he didn't seem to have. He chuckled, grinning down at the dog who would become a mother again.

Could it be true? Was this dog psychic? She would have the family she wanted?

"Her shots are up to date," the assistant said. "Her tag doesn't give a name. So, we'll leave that up to you. She's tolerated her food well; we'll send you home with a bag. Other than that, you're all set. If you don't have any questions, Tracy will check you out at the desk."

Annie couldn't answer. Her head spun from the shock of hearing a dog speak to her without barking. That had just happened—hadn't it?

When Annie didn't speak, Morgan answered for her. "We'll be fine."

"Call if you think of any questions after you get home. She should adjust to the puppies on her own. They're still so little, they won't have any trouble." The back door swung open once more. A young man, this time, carried Glenda, still wrapped in her kitchen towel.

Annie sat down on the kitchen's tile floor in front of her puppies, placing Glenda on the soft bed. On the ride home, they had decided on a name for their mother dog. Theresa now sniffed the puppies and wagged her tail as they cried out to her, telling her how much they needed her.

Annie held her breath.

Theresa circled the bed, sniffing each puppy in

turn, checking them. Then she looked at Annie as if to say okay. She lay down on one side of the dog bed, situating herself beside the puppies, and closed her eyes.

"I told you everything would be okay." Morgan placed a hand on the back of Annie's neck and massaged the tight muscles. "Dogs have been doing this a long time."

Annie took a deep breath as Glenda settled in with her new mother and some of the tension in her body unwound.

Mother's urn!

In all of the confusion, she'd left it in Morgan's truck. "My mother's..."

She hadn't even finished her sentence when Morgan spoke. "The urn is on the coffee table," he said softly. "I figured you'd want to find a place for it yourself."

Annie smiled up at him. "Thank you."

"It's past two already," he said. "How about some lunch?" Morgan slid the stale sandwiches left behind by Bryant on the kitchen table into the trash can.

"I'm not hungry." She sighed, wrapping her arms around her knees. Her entire body, exhausted from the ordeal, felt empty and drained.

"I'll fix your favorite, green salad with grilled chicken, boiled eggs, tomato, carrots, shredded cheddar, and Ranch dressing."

Annie laughed. "That's your favorite." But she had to admit that it sounded good. "Thanks." She started to get up.

"No." Morgan chuckled softly. "You stay right there with the puppies. I'll have it right up."

After lunch, Annie resumed her post beside the puppies while Morgan cleared away their dishes and put them into the dishwasher. He'd insisted. Warmth stole through her as she watched her husband's broad shoulders move about the kitchen. It hadn't taken her long after marrying Morgan to discover that firemen made great husbands, when they were around. She hoped this day could just keep on going the way it had. His phone had hardly rung once. And she looked forward to curling up next to him on the couch the way they used to, watching television, maybe even falling asleep that way. Her eyes ached to close even now.

Theresa was doing a great job with the puppies. They all slept as she vigilantly lay beside them.

Morgan shut off the water at the kitchen sink and turned to Annie. She could tell he had something on his mind, but his phone interrupted him.

Annie cringed inwardly at the sound she'd learned to dread. Her mind went automatically to the woman's name.

"It's an apartment fire," he said. "They need all off-duty personnel to come in."

"Will you just cover the station?"

"No, it looks like they need us to come to the scene."

"Be careful."

"I will." Morgan leaned down to give her a quick kiss on her lips.

Before she knew it, the front door closed behind him and the bolt slid shut. As she listened to his truck back down the driveway, large tires crunching shells beneath their heavy weight, sudden uneasiness stole over her, the way it did every time she found herself alone. She shivered with chill and fatigue. "Looks like it's just you and me and the puppies tonight, Theresa."

Theresa winked. The puppies were sleeping beside their surrogate mother.

Annie walked to the window in the front room. With Morgan's Landcruiser gone from the driveway, the house looked lonely. She took a deep breath as that familiar ache stole through her chest. First her father, then her mother, then Bryant, now her husband.

Suddenly the silence began to cut off her air. She couldn't stand there, waiting for Morgan to return, not when she knew that something was wrong. Something had not been right between her mother and her seeming friends.

One of them or all of them knows something about my mother that they aren't saying.

Annie had to find out what it was. She had to speak to them, but first she had to find them. Driven by her obsession and pure adrenaline, she knew just where to start.

The first thing Annie always noticed as she walked through the fire engine red door (painted so many times as to appear plastic) of The Solar Day Spa, passing through the waiting room lined with its vinyl chairs, coffee table full of tattered hair magazines, and coffee stand littered with used Equal packets and spilled coffee creamer, was the pungent scent of perm solution. As a kid, it had made her cringe, still did. There was just no getting used to the smell of something powerful enough to curl your hair or remove it, depending on your preference. She held her breath now as she passed the room responsible for the offensive aroma. A little gray-haired lady sat perched in a barber's chair beneath a plastic cape, reading a gossip magazine, her hair in small rollers.

An old house, the salon had been converted to a spa about four years ago, though Annie had always thought that *spa* was stretching it a bit. There were no massage tables or essential oils, not even soothing music piped in for effect, just light hits radio from the 70s and 80s. Everyone working for her there was a glorified hairdresser in a lab coat, nothing more.

Without stopping at the receptionist's desk, which was unmanned at the moment anyway, Annie marched straight to her mother's old room. She'd forgotten until that very moment, that it too, like her mother's condo, was full of knick-knacks. But as she walked down the hall to turn the corner into where her mother had cut hair for nearly three decades, over the sound of a distant hairdryer, she heard urgent voices drifting out.

"She found me at work. What was I supposed to say?" said a man's voice.

"What does she know?"

"Nothing, as far as I can tell."

"Well, you'd better be sure it stays that way and that you have an explanation ready. The police won't be too far behind."

"I know what I'm doing," a woman's voice said in defense. "They've already asked me what I know."

Annie took a step inside.

All three faces turned to her in unison, Henry Dekaretry, Nancy Carlucci, and Tab Weaver. Their open-mouthed faces stared at her until one had presence of mind enough to deflect.

"Little Annie Morgan," Nancy Carlucci said smoothly. "How nice to see you again. You all know Stella's daughter. Why we practically watched you grow up here."

Annie refused to take the bait. She wasn't about to be sucked in to a stroll down memory lane or to answer distracting questions about her husband's job. She said nothing until the silence stretched uncomfortably between them nearly snapping like a twig. Some of the group got fidgety.

"You're probably wondering what we're doing here," Henry Dekaretry said, taking the lead for his fellow conspirators.

Annie nodded, still saying nothing.

"This is our investor's group," he said. "We hold our monthly meetings here. And we didn't want to break with tradition. We thought your mother would appreciate that."

Tab Weaver cleared his throat. "I'm here on my mother's behalf, of course."

"I see," Annie said. Too shaken to ask questions, her tired brain scrambled for an excuse for her being there. "Well, please don't stop your meeting because of me. Continue on. I just came to collect my mother's things."

Three pairs of eyes followed her as Annie made a pretense of assessing the shelves full of six-inch porcelain pigs on point in tutus and erect dairy cows wearing evening gowns. Though without even a box to put them in, her deception quickly fell flat. She considered simply stuffing her purse full with as many as she could carry, but didn't want a farmyard full of broken animal bits by the time she got home.

"Well, I think we're all clear on what to do," Henry Dekaretry said to his group.

They all agreed unanimously.

"By the way, are you planning to sell your mother's spa now that she's no longer with us?" he said to Annie.

Annie's gaze narrowed on the man. "I hadn't really thought of it."

"Next month's meeting will have to be held somewhere else," he said. "And Mrs. Morgan will not be attendance then." His glare was pointed like a bull ready to charge.

Annie glanced over her shoulder. Everyone hurried out nearly knocking down Betty Vitkevich, who'd appeared in the doorway.

"Hello, Annie. I thought I heard Henry's dissenting voice coming from in here. Another one of their investor's club meetings, I see."

"Looks like it," Annie said.

"Don't let Henry bother you. He's just a blow-hard, but he's harmless really. Old age makes some of us crabby."

"I'll keep that in mind. I came here to speak to some of my mother's friends."

"But they had other things on their minds?" She ran a hand over her dark black pixie cut.

"You could say that."

"I'm here for a trim. Although I don't expect I'll ever get as good a cut again as I did from your mother. She really knew what she was doing. And she was such a good listener. I could tell her anything."

"That's very kind of you to say. But I could do with a little more from her. My mother seems to have had more secrets than truths. Mrs. Vitkevich, maybe you can clear something up for me. Calling what I just witnessed an investor's club seems to be a reach. Do they do anything besides pooling their money to buy lottery tickets?"

Betty Vitkevich smiled. "That's very perceptive of you. You know you're so very different from your mother." She tilted her head to one side and gazed at Annie. "For one thing, she kept everything close to the vest. Not like you, I can see by looking at your eyes that you wear your emotions on your sleeve. And I was listening at the door before."

"I take it that you aren't a part of the investor's club then?"

"Oh, no, dear. They kicked me out just like they kicked me out of the condo. To them, not having the funds every month is nearly as bad as having a dog." She laughed. "And there's another way you and your mother differ. If Henry had ever spoken to her the way he just spoke to you, she would've let him have it with both barrels."

"Maybe that has something to do with his hostility towards me."

"You never can tell. I remember the last time the two of them were in the same room. I was sitting under the dryer right here and Henry came in to ah, make his delivery."

"His delivery of what?"

"Uh, probably it was a lottery ticket for your

mother. Anyway, she said to him, 'Henry, when are you gonna let me do something about that hair of yours, what's left of it?'"

Betty laughed now. "Oh, we all had a good laugh at that. But not Henry. He never could laugh at himself."

"According to Henry, my mother owed the condo money."

"Oh, is that so?"

"You wouldn't remember ever hearing anything about that, would you?"

"Could've had something to do with the investor's club. She was a part of it."

"Did it?"

"Well, let me think. I seem to recall your mother mentioning one day that she'd better hide her checkbook or Henry Dekaretry would take every dime from her she had."

Annie waited, trying to hide her surprise.

"Yes. I remember now. It *was* for the investor's club. Once a month, they all pooled their social security money and Henry would buy the lottery tickets for them."

"What about Sarah Greis? Was she a part of their club too?"

"Yes, though she hasn't got the money the rest of them have, to throw away like that. She had to live off of her checks."

"Is that why she spends so much time with her son?"

"It could be. But she usually is only gone for a few weeks tops. Never this long."

"Is Mr. Dekaretry married?"

"No, he's a widower."

"How long ago did his wife die?"

"About three years ago."

"How did she pass?"

Betty scrunched up her nose, thinking. "Let's see, she had an inoperable brain tumor."

"Did she linger?"

"Well, yes, for a while. Why?"

"I want to get an idea about the kinds of people my mother was friends with. Sarah was on a fixed budget. Henry likely has hospital bills hanging over his head. Nancy was worried about losing a few lottery tickets."

"None of us have anything to hide, if that's what you mean."

"Everyone has something. What do you know about Tabbie Weaver's son?"

"Tab? He's a confirmed bachelor." Betty winked. "Never dated that I know of. But he's such a snappy dresser. Lives in a nice house not far from the condos. And he takes such good care of his mother."

"How is his mother? I knocked on her door but got no answer."

"That's probably because of her nose. She's very vain. And she hasn't got the money to back it up."

"How did she manage to break her nose playing with her grandkids?"

"Grandkids? She doesn't have any. Tab's an only child."

"He told me she broke her nose playing with her grandkids."

"Oh, he means," Betty hesitated, "uh, her new puppy."

Annie narrowed her gaze on the older woman, who was lying, or covering up, same thing.

The questions now were why was Tabbie Weaver really hiding? Why won't she answer her door? And Henry Dekaretry. Was his dislike of her mother strong enough to drive him to kill her? Or was it the money he needed? Then there was Mrs. Nancy Carlucci. Where does all of her money come from? Why does she care so much about lottery tickets? Next was Sarah Greis. Why has no one seen her lately? And what was her stuff doing at Goodwill? Finally, there was Betty Vitkevich standing right in front of her. How did she come to be kicked out of the condo and the club? Who ratted her out?

Before he'd left the house, Morgan had filled the back of his Landcruiser with the new airpacks from inventory in the garage. He hadn't wanted to forget about them. Lara's boss insisted on seeing one before committing to buying any, and Morgan hadn't known if he would get back home before his shift started in the morning. But he'd also gone upstairs to their bedroom for his duffel bag in case he had to sleep at the station tonight. And that's when he'd seen it. Annie had been very busy in the past few days, busier than he'd realized.

With his spare turnouts in the back of his truck, he'd driven straight to the fire without stopping first at his station for gear. The whole way there, all he could think about was what he'd seen in the nursery, that suspect poster Annie had created. Although he'd felt a great sense of satisfaction in seeing Bryant Smith's name among her list of suspects, none of it made any sense. She'd even gone so far as to include her old boss, Wade Biggins. Morgan was worried about her. He wished now he hadn't told her about Sarah Greis' extraordinary death. Had this all been too much for her? Was she not able to cope with the reality of losing her mother and that's why she was doing it? Suspecting everyone her mother had known of possibly being her murderer, wasn't that paranoia?

Morgan parked now in front of the brick apartment building. Visible smoke rose from an upper floor apartment.

Eddie spotted his truck and walked over in full turnouts. "I see you've got those new airpacks you told me about."

"Lighter by a few pounds and a narrower profile. A lot of departments I've talked with want them for their RITs. I'm trying to talk Chief Gant into buying a dozen to start. He already let me fill a few of them for demonstration."

"Sounds good to me. I'm getting too old to haul around any extra weight."

Morgan made a sound of disbelief as Eddie patted his own still flat stomach. He had his turnout pants on the ground with the boots sitting inside them. He stepped into both at the same time, pulling the pants up by the suspenders. He shrugged into his turnout jacket.

Since he hadn't been able to have that talk with Annie at home, he pulled out his phone now and began texting. His fingers pressed all the wrong buttons and auto correct filled in the wrong words. Finally, he gave up and tossed his phone onto the seat of his truck. It would have to wait. In person tonight would be better than a text anyway.

Annie lay on the living room sofa, curled up on her side, unable to sleep. Her conversation with Betty Vitkevich replayed in her tired mind like a broken record. She wanted to put all of the pieces of the puzzle together, but her exhausted brain wouldn't let her.

The light had shifted inside the house by the time Annie heard a car on the shell-covered drive. She flew to the window. The setting sun obscured her vision, but it wasn't Morgan she saw returning home from a canceled call as she'd hoped.

Bryant stepped out of a different taxi, and he carried his luggage.

Annie leaned against the open door. "What happened? Miss your plane?"

Bryant didn't smile, didn't make eye contact with her at all. He walked past her into the living room.

"What are you doing back here?"

"I'd think that would be obvious. Morgan interrupted us. He's gone now."

"Yes, he's on a call. How did you know that?"

With a smile that didn't reach his eyes, Bryant produced his cell phone. "It's an app that monitors police and fire department's radio traffic. I always know where Morgan is. You should get one too."

Chills ran over Annie's body. "How long have you had that?"

"Years."

That explained how Bryant had always stayed one step ahead of Morgan, popping up whenever Morgan left and leaving just before he arrived.

"I don't need it. I trust my husband."

Bryant chuckled. "That's always been your trouble. You're too trusting. Like those scars. You wouldn't have them if you hadn't been so naïve. I told you you couldn't trust him either."

Annie flinched. "Some of us learn our lessons the hard way."

"It didn't have to be that way. It could've been you and me from the beginning."

"Bryant, you and I *have* been from the beginning, but nothing ever happened between us. You never even tried to kiss me. Doesn't that tell you anything?"

"Yes, that I have too much respect for you to paw all over you like a silly teenager."

Annie shook her head. "Despite it all, you still make Morgan jealous."

Bryant smiled a genuine smile this time. "Good."

"I wouldn't go that far. I can understand how he might've gotten the wrong idea about us."

"Whatever he thought about us, he was right to. I've wanted to steal you away from him since the moment he stepped into my place. What do you think it did to me, watching him get closer and closer to my best friend? Watching him steal the woman I'd invested so much time into. Marrying you. Buying this house."

"This all comes as a great shock to me. You've never said any of this before."

"How could I, with you so in love?" The last word had come out dripping with sarcasm. Bryant's eyes were round and color rose high on his cheeks.

"Bryant, I think your vision is a little skewed right now. You're in the middle of a big transition in your life with the year abroad. Go back to Italy. Make the best of your time there, and when you get back, if you still want to, you and I can still be friends."

Bryant hadn't heard her. He rubbed at the back of his neck. "You two with your matching watches and SUVs and now a freaking litter of puppies. You both make me sick."

Annie's mouth fell open. "I think you should go back to Italy now."

This wasn't the man she'd known. If he lashed out at her now, she wouldn't be surprised. But he didn't. He turned on his heel, picked up his suitcase, and walked out.

Annie's whole body convulsed as the front door slammed. She paced the living room and kitchen without ever seeing that Bryant's taxi had not waited for him.

She couldn't settle her mind. The silence of the house surrounded her, choking her.

Theresa's blue and brown eyes followed her.

Finally, Annie couldn't stand the solitude one more second. She kissed the top of Theresa's head. "I'll be back in about twenty minutes."

Theresa lifted her head to look directly into Annie's eyes.

Annie glanced at the clock on the wall. "At eight o'clock, okay?"

Theresa closed her eyes, rested her head back down on the bed, and sighed.

Annie could have sworn she heard "okay".

Morgan got the radio call from Eddic saying that he needed to come back out. A supply hose connected to the hydrant had burst and the engineer had to put in another two sections of hose because the dry hose would not be stretched like the already wet hose was. He hadn't noticed how much time had passed since he'd walked in. The apartment would be a total loss; he could see that much through the gray smoke.

As soon as he was clear, he removed his face mask and airpack, carrying his helmet in his hand. He walked to the pumper truck where Taylor fitted a STORZ connection, a large diameter supply line, to the truck from the hydrant. The whole building was involved. Half of the work being done at the moment was spraying the adjacent buildings with the water hoses to prevent them from catching fire as well.

Since he hadn't reached Annie to say that he'd gotten there safely and would be there for quite a while, he would call her now and tell her to go to bed, that he would wake her when he got home.

At his Landcruiser, over the shouting of orders, the wind, the roar of the fire, and the boom of the pumper truck, Morgan used his flash light to find his cell phone in the back seat of his truck where it had landed. He stuck a finger in one ear and pressed the phone to his other.

The male voice that answered Annie's phone was not the voice he'd expected to hear.

"Bryant?" Morgan's heart felt like it would pound out of his chest. In the space of a few seconds, he'd pictured a million life-threatening scenarios. "Where the hell is Annie?"

Eddie Stanton, Incident Commander, stood nearby as Morgan shouted into his phone.

Finally hanging up, he threw it into the back seat

of his truck.

"Finally reach Annie?"

Morgan leaned against the Landcruiser and shook his head, not looking at his friend.

"Is she okay?"

"It's over."

Eddie, who had removed his turnout jacket, crossed his arms over his chest. "It's not over til it's over."

Morgan's brow creased. "Save your horseshit for someone who needs it."

"Did she say it was over?"

"Look, what am I supposed to think? She's with him every time my back is turned."

"Is she? Or does he show up every time your back is turned?"

Morgan started to answer then looked at Eddie as realization dawned.

"You're scared of public speaking aren't you, buddy?"

Morgan scowled at him. "What?"

"Answer me," Eddie shouted over the din.

"You know I am."

"Scares you more than anything doesn't it, more than suiting up in all this gear, strapping an air tank on your back, breathing artificial air, and walking into a building on fire?"

Morgan gave him a level look. "You know the answer."

"Humor me."

"Yes, public speaking scares me more than anything else."

"What scares Annie more than anything?"

"Eddie, we don't have time for this right now."

"You've got time. I sent in Taylor and Nicky to relieve you. Now just answer the question."

Morgan heaved a sigh. "Being alone."

"And how do you know that? Remember what you told me?"

He did. The first shift after they were married, Annie had gone to her mother's condo to sleep for the night. Then every shift after that, she'd done the same, until her mother finally told her enough was enough. She was married to a fireman and would have to get used to being alone.

Morgan looked at the ground where even in the dark he could see the water that ran past his feet was black with debris from the fire. "I never thought about it that way."

"You're here risking your life, and she's at home waiting for you to come back to her. And she doesn't know if one day, you won't come back."

Morgan shook his head. "She's never said anything even remotely close to that."

"She wouldn't. She's not the type. On the outside, she's got her shit together. Career. Home." Eddie raised his index finger. "But she *thinks* it. I guarantee you, she thinks it."

"No, she's off on some wild goose chase, apparently trying to prove that someone murdered her mother, if you can believe that."

"Amazing how the mind works, isn't it?"

"Eddie, this philosophical side of you is truly pissing me off."

"What's truly amazing are the things we humans will do to distract ourselves from thinking about what's really bothering us. Becky always wanted to keep chickens, but even though we had the land, I never got around to building her a coop. After she left me, I started building them like crazy."

Morgan shook his head, partially at his friend who wouldn't leave him alone and partly at the ridiculous memory. "I remember that. You built so many of those things, you had to give them away."

Eddie nodded. "And my point is this, I did it because thinking about what had been wrong with my marriage was more than I could handle. Building chicken coops gave me something to do that was tangible, kept my brain from overthinking."

"And you're saying that's what Annie is doing."

"Being a Math teacher, her mind is probably reeling with possibilities and strategizing formulas to solve this problem. She needs more than anything to know that one plus one still equals two. You leaving her for some bimbo in a tight skirt, in her mind, doesn't make sense, because you two love each other, because she trusts you."

"I'm *not* leaving her," Morgan growled.

Eddie put up his hands in surrender. "Then don't tell me. Tell her."

Chapter 9

Bryant watched in the dark from the corner of the cottage as Annie walked down to the shore. When she got there she would remove her clothes and drop them onto the dry sand before she dove into the water. She still had not let go of the mermaid she had been when she'd met Morgan. His body reacted to the image that appeared in his mind. If he walked down to the shore, there would be nothing but rejection waiting for him. He'd always known that once he'd revealed his feelings, he'd see pity in her eyes, the kind of pity he'd seen tonight. He'd come close to telling her years ago after she'd broken up with the Neanderthal she'd called her boyfriend before Morgan. The night the Neanderthal had attacked her, he'd planned to take her out to dinner and finally tell her the truth. Instead, she'd called him up from work to tell him that she'd met the man she was going to marry.

He could still kill her for it.

Instead of following her, he walked into Morgan's garage and found an empty box with a picture of bananas stamped on the side.

If he couldn't have Annie, he'd take her most valuable possession from her. He would take from her what she wanted as much as he wanted her. Her family. He strolled through the front door he'd just left.

She wants a family, then a litter of puppies falls into her lap.

How fair is that?

This would even things between them.

"I can't have her; she can't have a family."

To his delight as he entered the kitchen, Annie's phone, which sat on the table, rang. Bryant smiled to himself as he answered the call from the great Chance Morgan.

"She's not dressed at the moment. And she's in no condition to come to the phone right now. Can I give her a message?"

Bryant smiled to himself as he listened to Morgan's angry reply.

"I'll tell her." Bryant hung up and laughed. It had been too easy.

With a green dry erase marker, he wrote on the white board that hung from Annie's refrigerator.

Bryant packed the sleeping puppies one at a time inside the cardboard box while the dog glared at him, growling. By the last one, she had bared her teeth and tried to bite him. She followed him, barking. He had just made it to the front door, carrying the puppies, when the mother dog's teeth hooked his pants leg. He kicked backwards, forcing her back inside and slammed the door shut in her face.

Why should Annie have everything when because of her, now he had nothing?

Morgan had noticed that the apartment unit next door started releasing smoke from its roof line even before Eddie began waving to him from the yard. That meant that the prevention had not worked and the unit next to the fire's origin had caught fire as well.

Morgan had been the first to go in. He and Nicky Pilgrim, a rookie by comparison, had climbed onto the roof to vent the heat. They didn't want heat building up to the point of flashover if they could prevent it. Morgan had Nicky now pointing the infrared camera all over the interior, scanning for trapped victims. In an apartment fire, the variables were too many, too many residents to assume that no one had been left behind. Children too often were known to hide in closets or under beds to try to escape fires. He wouldn't take any chances.

"All clear, Lieutenant."

Morgan motioned for Nicky to follow him up the exterior metal stairs that led to the upper floor apartments. They had just swept the two ground floor apartments and found nothing. Morgan prayed that the upper two proved the same.

The door to Morgan's left had a door mat that read, "Wipe Your Paws". Someone's dog may be trapped inside. Then he thought again of Annie. She'd never had a family of her own, not even so much as a pet. Despite his anger, his heart ached for her pain.

Annie dove into the darkened water. It cooled her overheated skin, clearing her mind and focusing her thoughts. When she surfaced, she turned to her cottage. The light remained on in the kitchen. Theresa and the puppies were safe. Annie dove under the waves. Tonight she would swim out past where the waves broke, far enough that she could still see her home, but far enough that she became once more the mermaid she'd been. Her mother had been alive then, a happy, healthy, vital woman, until someone had snuffed out her light.

Only Morgan mattered to her now. She'd walked away from her career without so much as a hesitation, and she'd not suffered a moment's regret. But without Morgan she didn't have a life. Every minute she'd spent shopping and eating out with Bryant had taken something away from her marriage. Morgan was right; they didn't need to go away to be together. They just needed to find a way to reconnect, to find the reason they'd been drawn together in the first place. But how could she even think about a honeymoon when her mother's killer roamed free?

Annie pushed further and further out, forcing herself to hold her breath longer and longer each time she dove. She wouldn't panic the way she had before. This time, she would see just how far she could go. The water rushing past her skin transformed her into who she needed to be. She dove once, twice, then three times, each time, going past the point she'd ever gone before. When she finally surfaced, her house shined like a dot on the shore, still there, but only as a marker so she could find her way back. She could always find her way back, no matter how far she went.

She turned toward shore now, knowing she had left her old self behind, the confused, uncertain Annie. The tide had carried her out to sea, never to return. New Annie had a purpose, to help those without a voice, her mother, her puppies, no matter what form they took. At that moment, she heard in her mind a desperate cry for help. It had not come from any human, no voice. Theresa. It had come from Theresa. She cried out from the house where Annie had left her. Again, as she had in the vet's office, Theresa used her mind to communicate with Annie. She had not used audible words that Annie would hear with her ears but words she heard in her heart, the way she'd heard her say the word family.

Annie swam as fast as she could back to the beach and back to her home where Theresa's heart cried out to hers.

Mouths gaped as Nicky rushed out of the apartment fire alone.

"Three-four-seven, request acknowledgment."

No response.

Eddie pressed the radio's button harder this time. "Talk to me, Morgan!" he yelled into the mouthpiece.

Nicky removed his helmet and turnout jacket. With his shirt's sleeve, he wiped trails of sweat from his forehead and eyes. He and the assistant chief stood alongside Eddie now, waiting impatiently as well for a response from Morgan.

Assistant Chief Watts turned to Nicky. "What happened in there?"

"The fire is bigger than we thought," he said between breaths, "like somebody used an accelerant."

"That confirms what we've been hearing from some residents." Eddie nodded to the chief. "They're saying they smelled gasoline right before they saw the smoke."

"Morgan went into one of the bedrooms. He ran out, signaling me to go out ahead of him. I thought he was right behind me."

"Did his PASS alarm sound?"

"No, sir."

"If Morgan doesn't respond within the next ten seconds, I want Taylor suited up and inside."

Eddie turned to the assistant chief. "Taylor's running the pumper truck. And he's green. I'll go in."

"Okay, Eddie. Just remember, Morgan's wearing the same airpack he went in with. He's been inside more than thirty minutes."

"Last chance, Morgan." Eddie pressed the button on his radio once more. "Three-four-seven, acknowledge!" He shook his head. "Still no answer."

"You're up, Stanton."

Eddie's turn outs waited for him on the back of Engine 2. He had the process down to about ten seconds. This one took him five. With his helmet securely in place, he tapped one of the firefighters staging in front of the building, standing by for their turn inside the fire. As they assisted each other into their airpacks, Eddie began to explain the situation.

"I know," the firefighter said, "We've all been listening. We're ready."

Moments later, the two of them walked into the burning building.

Annie breast stroked back to shore, every muscle in her body straining with the effort. She kept her house in sight. The undertow had sent her down shore so that her cottage now sat to her right. She ignored the alarm bells that sounded in her head.

Every stroke of her arms to reach her way out of the water converged with the force of the ocean pulling her back in. She had finally pushed too far. This time, she wouldn't make it back to shore. Her leg muscles were as heavy as concrete. Only Theresa's cry for help kept her arms and legs moving.

Her breaths came in gasps but still she kept going. She slid farther and farther away from her home. Then in a moment of weakness, she let her legs rest. The tug of the undertow pulled her down with it. Just before the sight of home disappeared, she took a last gasp of air.

Morgan had not taken the time to swap airpacks before going back in. He had enough left on the pack he wore to do a visual sweep for victims potentially trapped inside the fire. Fortunately, so far, he'd found none, not even the four-legged kind.

Children and animals potentially trapped inside had kept Morgan from turning back. The last room, a bedroom with a bunkbed, held stuffed animals and matchbox cars but not children at the moment. Convinced now no one remained inside the apartment, he turned for the door. But at that moment, the floor beneath him splintered. He ran, motioning for Nicky to get out ahead of him. He felt more than heard the floor collapse beneath him. His leg slipped into a crack between floor joists. He fell backwards onto his airpack, his leg trapped between the subfloor and the ceiling below. Pinned on his back, he looked up but could only see in his mind Annie. He had to get back to her. She had to know that he had always been faithful, never even considered another woman. She was all he'd ever wanted. And she needed to hear him say it.

Eddie and his partner didn't make it all the way up the exterior stairway before hearing Morgan's

PASS alarm's shrill shrieking—Morgan wasn't moving. They had to move fast. Through the thick black smoke, they could see that the second floor apartment had collapsed. A couch dangled in midair above them, half on and half off the floor, two of its feet held in place by one of the bare floor joists that made up the first floor apartment's ceiling. They could see straight up into the living room. Morgan should have at least made it that far, but he was nowhere in sight. Eddie grabbed the infrared camera hanging from his turnout jacket, using it to scan the area for Morgan. At the same time, he followed the sound of the alarm. From his perch mid-way up the flight of metal stairs, he shined the camera into the apartment that Morgan and Nicky had just been inside. Through the camera's lens, all around him were blacks, blues, greens, yellows, and reds. The ceiling, where the heat collected the fastest, turned the yellow color of a lemon. Where the fire burned the hottest he saw the color of a red flame. A coffee table, not on fire, in the center of the room appeared black. He spotted another black image, not a part of the contents of the apartment, letting him know he'd found Morgan. Without the camera, he could just make out a corner of a turnout jacket beneath a turned over bookcase.

"I see him," Eddie yelled though only as audible as a whisper to his partner.

"Let's go!"

Eddie shook his head. "There's only room for one person to reach him."

"That floor could give the rest of the way any minute," his partner shouted.

Without another thought, Eddie nimbly climbed the rest of the way up. The landing at the top of the stairs remained intact, for now. Using the floor joists for support, he pulled himself up into the gaping floor of the apartment. Morgan's body lay about ten feet from the open doorway where the floor remained partially intact. Eddie crawled on hands and knees to his friend's motionless body and lay his head on Morgan's right shoulder. No movement, no sound of the airpack.

Before turning to come back out, he motioned to his partner to let him know he was coming down. Leaving Morgan where he lay grated every fiber of Eddie's being, but with his plan solidified in his mind, he knew now what he had to do.

Pulled under by the invisible force below, Annie had finally pushed too far. A strong swimmer, she'd become overconfident. She had never considered, never even thought this could happen to her, and here it had. Her mind became a swirl of unrelated thought, memories. She could see her mother on the day Annie had married Morgan. She hugged her mother. Then turning to Morgan, she reached out a hand to him, to let him know that she still wanted him. But he vanished. She frantically looked around but could not see him. Suddenly the roar of the ocean surrounding her became a black, smoke-filled fire, raging. Morgan was inside, trapped just as surely as the undertow had trapped her.

All the times she'd seen Morgan frustrated, working on one of the trucks he'd rebuilt by hand, he'd never given up. He'd become so angry replacing the rear axle seals that he'd cursed a blue streak. Even with every bolt rusted into place he never quit, despite having to remove both brake drums to even get at the old seals. He'd come inside the house after hours and hours of work in the garage, covered in black oil and grease, smiling because he'd finally done it. And riding in the back of that ambulance with her, looking down at her face and smiling, he hadn't let her quit. He hadn't even let her close her eyes.

For one brief second, Lara's image appeared in her mind. If she gave up and let the blackness swallow her, Lara would move in on her husband. She wouldn't let that happen.

With every muscle in her body tensed and ready to fight, she climbed her way up and up until finally she broke the surface of the water. Free now, she took a deep breath and forced her body to relax. Everything she'd ever read about the undertow had said not to fight it. Forcing herself to surrender to the water was the hardest thing she'd ever had to do, but she willed her arms and legs to drift up to the surface of the water. Her body in line now with her head and shoulders, she floated, fighting the urge to kick her legs. The stillness became spiritual, and she drifted. All she had to do to save her own life was stop fighting and let the tide do the rest.

Eddie stood at the open hatch of Morgan's Landcruiser, looking inside at the small collection of airpacks. He grabbed one of the new, filled bottles and removed it from its box. Using it was something he could get into a lot of trouble over because it didn't belong to the department, wasn't standard equipment.

But he preferred bending the rules to regret.

The ladder truck sprayed all around them now. Steam hissed and spat as it landed on the overheated brick. Only it and support beams of the original building remained standing. But the chief had been advised that Morgan was trapped inside the adjacent building. They could not and would not spray it until he was out of harm's way.

Like a sprinter, Eddie rushed back into the stairwell and up the flight of metal stairs once again. As he did, his rubber soled boots stuck to each step due to the intense heat. Four of Morgan's fellow firemen in full airpacks followed behind Eddie as he climbed higher into the heat and smoke, prepared to carry him down the stairs and into safety.

When he reached him, Eddie forced his shaking gloved hands to remove Morgan's air hose, something that went against all common sense, but had to be done. Because Morgan lay on his back, Eddie could not reach his air tank. He had to remove the mask Morgan wore, something that had to be done quickly. The air tank gauge on Morgan's shoulder read empty. Eddie had to swap out the airpacks. As he attached his friend's regulator to the new lightweight air tank, he blessed Morgan and his side business. He'd told Morgan he was crazy to try to make a living selling fire equipment wholesale to fire departments. He'd never been so happy to be wrong. He opened the valve to start the fresh oxygen then motioned to the awaiting firefighters.

Each of the five men supported Morgan's weight, but not easily. Required workouts and routine trainings had never been more appreciated than at that moment as Eddie along with the four others lifted Morgan's motionless body and carried him down the stairs.

Annie emerged from the water and picked up her clothes. On her run across the sand flicking against her calves, and all the way back to her house, the thought that something was very wrong there screamed at her. Her imagination conjured the worst, Morgan hurt, the puppies, her house. She flung open the back door and heard Theresa whining in the living room. Glenda's puppies weren't in their bed in the kitchen. Annie could see Theresa pacing. There were visible marks on the front door where Theresa had obviously tried to scratch it open.

Bryant. She had just told him that she didn't love him. Angry at her, he'd taken them to punish her.

Annie's chest tightened. The precious little puppies, completely dependent on her and Theresa for their survival had been taken.

"Why would Bryant do this? To get back at me? Why not yell or scream?"

From the front door, Theresa turned, looking to Annie. The whimper she let out was sobering.

"You're right. I don't have time to ask why. We have to get your puppies back."

Theresa went back to trying to pry open the door with her claws and Annie picked up her phone to call Morgan. A message on the white board caught her eye, written in Bryant's hand.

Tell Annie I won't be home tonight or any other night.

"Morgan?" Annie choked out the word.

She looked down at the phone in her hand. She had no one to call—no husband, no mother, no father, no friend. The family Theresa had promised her crumbled around her. Truly alone for the first time in her life, her thoughts raced. Her heart doubled its rhythm. No! She refused to give in.

Morgan, angry or not, would help her find Theresa's puppies. Even if their marriage was over, he would still assist her. He'd tried to tell her in so many ways.

"Annie, you didn't have to do that alone. I would've gone with you."

"Why didn't you tell me about your mother? I would've come right home."

"I would've come home and taken care of Glenda."

Trying to do everything alone was where she'd gone wrong. When her mother died, she'd handled it alone. When Glenda died, she'd handled it alone. Morgan had offered to solve all of her problems for her, but she hadn't heard him. He wanted to make her life as effortless as he could because that's the kind of man he was.

She dialed Morgan's station. The same deep voice, that she didn't know but remembered, answered. "Station Two."

"Could you please tell me where Lieutenant Morgan is?"

"Jacksonville Apartments. Who's this?"

"His wife." Annie hung up, a surge of energy filling her.

Her heart raced but not from fear anymore. She would go to him. She had to. She had to tell him what he needed to know. She wasn't giving up on them. She needed him.

The GPS on her phone guided her to the apartment complex downtown. But as she drove, she began to worry more and more about the missing puppies out there somewhere, alone, without their mother. The vet had told her to call if she had any problems. She had to call someone, anyone. Her hands shook as she dialed. The answering machine picked up on the fourth ring. She hung up. Her fingers had pressed 9-1 before she stopped herself.

What am I thinking?

She spotted the apartment building long before GPS told her she'd arrived. Thick smoke darker than the night sky filled the air. Flashing lights whirled, casting an eerie glow over the brick buildings. The water from the hoses had blanketed the scene with a dense black fog. And as she got closer, she could see the brilliant orange flames consume one entire building.

Annie parked her Landcruiser next to Morgan's, relieved to find it there. When she got out, she could see that Ladder Truck 2 shot water from its peak. It sizzled and crackled as it rained down. Annie walked as far as she could towards the apartment building. The police had put up a yellow tape barrier between the parking lot and playground, keeping spectators on the grass. Between the noise of the trucks and the crowds of onlookers. Annie couldn't hear herself think let alone spot a familiar face.

She found a police officer. "I've got to get through. My husband is one of the firefighters."

"Ma'am, you're going to have to stay on that side

with everyone else. No one's getting through."

"But I've got to talk to him. It's important."

The sheriff's deputy shook his head.

"I've got to!" But she might as well have been talking to a brick wall. He didn't say another word and turned his back on her.

Red, blue, and white strobe lights lit up the parking lot of the apartment complex. Paramedics waited for the five firemen at the bottom of the stairs, as close to the fire as they could get without airpacks of their own.

As soon as the five of them were within arm's length of the awaiting paramedics, they took over, placing Morgan's body on a gurney. The wheels were sprung beneath him and they wheeled him to the awaiting ambulance.

The paramedics walked and at the same time removed Morgan's airpack, the one that had saved his life.

Eddie watched and removed his own airpack, taking his first deep breath since the night had begun. He climbed in next to the two paramedics.

"His heart rate is 100 bpms," one of them said.

He had a heart beat; that's all Eddie needed to know.

Medical scissors were too small to cut through Morgan's turnout jacket. So the arduous task of removing it began. Morgan's t-shirt, soaked in perspiration, clung to his chest. One of the paramedics swabbed Morgan's now bare arm with isopropyl alcohol and started a saline IV. His turnout pants were also removed and the second paramedic looked for injuries, finding none. Through all of it, Morgan did not regain consciousness.

The assistant chief arrived at the back of the ambulance before it could leave the crowded parking lot. "How is he?"

"Heart and lungs are working," Eddie said. "No injuries. He's still out."

"Have you called his wife?"

Eddie shook his head. "I can't do it to her."

"I'll call her." The assistant chief pulled his phone from his pocket. "She doesn't know me. It will be easier coming from a stranger."

Still waiting to catch a glimpse of Morgan from behind the barricade, Annie's phone vibrated in her pocket. A number showed that she didn't recognize.

"Annie, this is Simon Watts, the assistant chief of Eastview Fire Department."

Annie's heart stopped then began to beat wildly.

"Morgan's being sent to Hillcrest Hospital."

The words stuck in her throat but she finally forced them through dry lips. "Is he okay?"

"Can you meet me there?" The man's tone was sympathetic, which only served to further her alarm.

"I'm here, behind the police tape." She didn't recognize the sound of her own voice. "I can see the ambulance. Is that Morgan?" she cried out the last three words.

Annie reminded herself to take slow breaths as she marched towards the ambulance, the whole dreamlike scene moving around her. The people she passed by seemed to disappear along with all sound except the thundering of her own heart. He wouldn't make it. She would never have his children. They would never be a family. Theresa had said to her—family. It could've all been for nothing, some cosmic lesson she'd failed.

She followed the ambulance down the busy streets to the hospital. When they arrived at the over-lit emergency entrance, she found a parking spot easily. Getting out of the truck without falling on her face proved the difficulty. Her arms and legs shook with each forced step. She walked inside alone, asked the desk nurse to see her husband, and was told she would have to take a seat until called. She looked around the waiting area for a familiar face but once again found herself alone.

She sat down next to a potted Yarrow plant. Scenes from her seven-year marriage sprang to her mind as though she watched a movie. Morgan in his tux on their wedding day. She'd never seen a more handsome figure. The countless nights they'd spent on the couch together in their pajamas, eating Chinese take-out, making love at the drop of a hat because of a certain way he'd looked into her eyes or kissed her neck or touched her cheek. There had been a time when they hadn't been able to get enough of each other, when she hadn't been able to get enough of him. They had been more than lovers; they'd been friends.

"You found us."

She looked up and saw Eddie Stanton standing in front of her. She nodded.

"I'm sorry I wasn't here to greet you. I'm pretty grimy from the fire."

Annie barely noticed how different Eddie looked

tonight, his hair damp from perspiration, the creases of his forehead covered in soot, faint red lines around his mouth and eyes from his air mask. She opened her mouth to ask what had happened but the words didn't come.

Eddie looked down into her eyes and tilted his head to one side. An innocent gesture of sympathy, but it sent shock waves through Annie.

"Is he?"

She didn't have to finish her sentence.

"No!"

Her face collapsed and a torrent of tears poured from her eyes.

Eddie who'd never been anything but a gentleman suddenly pulled her to him and wrapped her in a strong embrace from her head where his hand rested atop her hair all the way to her feet where the tips of his boots pressed against her bare toes in her sandals. Maybe loyalty did go the other way. For a moment she relished the safety of his arms and his chest pressed against her. But she had to know. She pulled back and looked up at him. "What happened?"

Eddie released her, looking down into her eyes. "Morgan is unconscious right now, Annie."

A cold shaft stabbed her middle.

"He breathed in a little smoke. But he's stable. He's going to be okay."

"Can I see him?"

Inside the pale blue room Morgan had been taken to, a heart monitor beeped. The sound echoed off the painted cement block walls.

"We've given him something to help him sleep,"

the nurse said to Annie. "So, he'll be in and out for a while, but he can hear you." The nurse drew the curtain, the metal rings scraping the rod as she left the room.

An IV dripped into a clear tube that led to the crook of Morgan's arm and Annie sat down beside it on a vinyl chair. A framed print hung over the bed of the Archangel Michael holding a sword in one hand and pointing the way with the other. She leaned over towards the edge of Morgan's bed, resting her forearms on the mattress.

His pale face looked exhausted. Dark skin ringed his eyes. She pulled a tube of Burt's Bees from her purse and rubbed some of the clear peppermint balm over his dry lips.

His eyes fluttered beneath closed lids.

The warmth of the room and the quiet of the night combined to make the desire to close her own eyes nearly overwhelming. Her body felt heavy, exhausted from caring for the puppies nights instead of sleeping. She felt herself drifting. Suddenly, her whole body convulsed. Her eyes popped open. Morgan still hadn't moved. She held his hand.

"Don't you dare leave me alone here with your mother." The words had just tumbled out of her mouth of their own volition.

She caught Morgan's slight grin. He tried to squeeze her hand but couldn't. His closed eyes shifted beneath their lids as he went back to wherever he had been.

Annie let herself cry now. Without Morgan, she had only herself, no family, as Theresa had said. And worse, she'd missed her chance at the life she'd been given. She lightly stroked his cheek with the back of her finger. "I'm sorry for every time I didn't answer my phone when you called me because I was mad at you. And I'm sorry for pretending to be asleep sometimes when you came home late at night after you'd been gone all day. I'm also sorry that I let myself get consumed with my mother's death. I got so far gone, I even thought she'd been murdered."

Annie watched Morgan's closed eyelids flutter, but his body remained still.

"What happened to us?" she said.

His eyes still remained closed.

She silently pleaded with him to answer her, to open his eyes and say something even if to argue.

"I'll tell you my theories. And if you disagree, speak up."

No reply came from Morgan's lips.

Annie's voice was a whisper, but she needed to talk even if to herself. "I think it all started on our wedding day. Your mother wouldn't smile. Do you remember? She looked like someone had robbed her of her one and only happiness. I'm pretty sure that was you. The one picture I have of her and me in the bride's room of the church, she isn't even trying to smile. I've always found that odd. Maybe she couldn't. Maybe she thought that if she did, it would encourage me. And she let me know constantly and without fail all of the things I was doing wrong. My hair is too thick. Women my age shouldn't have so much hair. I guess I should get mine cut off like hers?"

Annie waited, but Morgan lay still unmoving. A cold shaft stabbed at her middle again. But she tried to push it away.

"Do you remember the time that your sister sent us that barbeque invitation?"

He didn't stir.

"I got the invitation in the mail while you were on duty. The date fell on your birthday, and, of course, you were on duty that day anyway. So, we couldn't go even if we'd wanted to. I called her and told her I was sorry we couldn't make it. Somehow she didn't get the message. The party rolled around and we weren't there. She didn't speak to me for a month after that but never told me why. And you and I ended up getting into that huge argument. Once the both of you weren't speaking to me, I thought I'd go crazy."

Annie sighed.

"Am I crazy to let stuff like that get to me?" She tapped her own chest. "I mean, she's an adult too. Why not just come right out and tell me instead of assuming I'd lied to her?"

Annie held her head in her hands.

"Maybe that's what got my mother into trouble; she never questioned her friend's integrity."

The sound of a tray in the hallway crashing to the floor snapped her back to attention. Annie got up and poured herself a glass of water from the faucet. She took one sip and slammed the cup down on the counter.

"Of course, your sister didn't call me a liar outright. Nooo. She never says anything outright. There's just those subtle hints and insinuations that don't hit their mark until you see the back of her head on her way out the door."

She sat back down beside Morgan. "I promise not to let anything ever take me away from you again, not a best friend, not a dog, not finding a killer, not even hurt from your sister. You're all that matters."

The nurse breezed into the room on silent feet, pushing the noisy curtain aside. Morgan didn't stir. Without looking at Annie, she checked Morgan's IV and his heart rate, making note of it on the clipboard that hung from the foot of the bed.

"If he wakes up, he may have water." The nurse nodded to the pink pitcher and cup that sat beside the bed. "No food until the doctor checks him."

Annie nodded. On her way out the nurse glanced at Annie. She left as quickly as she'd come.

Annie could see her own reflection in the mirror above the sink. She looked as crazed as she felt.

Annie looked around the room. A framed print of a field of chamomile flowers hung on the wall above a club chair, the only other chair in the room besides the hard plastic one she currently sat on. She rested her head on her arms on the edge of the mattress beside Morgan's head and felt very tired. She closed her eyes. In her mind, she weighed the good with the bad. Their marriage had been good because they were good together, not that they'd been good in a long time. All of the hurt had been left to fester.

Had they gone too far to turn back?

Chapter 10

Minutes later a different nurse pulled the curtain back slowly so that it didn't scrape the way it had the times before, leaving in her wake a trail of gardenia blossoms as she crossed the room.

A faint light from outside peeked in through the slats of the vertical blinds. Annie checked her watch on her wrist. Seven o'clock. It had been hours she'd been asleep, not minutes.

She stretched and yawned as the nurse went through her check of Morgan, this one more thorough. She took his pulse with her own hands and wrote it down. She took his temperature with a digital ear thermometer. She checked his eyes for dilation. All of this without waking him.

"The doctor turned off his IV drip about an hour ago," the nurse said to Annie.

She must have slept right through that.

"So, he should be waking up soon. When he does, call me and I'll have his breakfast sent up to him. There's a snack counter one door down. You're welcome to help yourself."

As soon as the nurse left the room, Morgan's eyelids opened. Relief washed over her.

She reached for his hand and his bloodshot eyes found hers. He looked at her face, her neck, her shoulders. "Have you been eating, Ann? You look too thin." His voice was hoarse and groggy but had never sounded so good.

Annie smiled. She buried her face against his neck where his beard stubble chafed her lips. His hand still bound by the IV caressed the back of her head.

When he tried to sit up, Annie pressed a hand against his chest. "No, don't try to move. Here, let me adjust the bed for you." The bed inched upward at an excruciating pace until finally, Morgan and Annie could see eye to eye. When Annie stopped the movement, Morgan took over the button and lifted the bed up the rest of the way.

She smiled at the boyish look on his face. "You've always been a terrible patient."

"I know. I wanted to see you."

"I'm right here. I'm not going anywhere."

"Promise?" he said.

"Promise."

"When I called home last night, Bryant answered."

"I figured as much when I read your message."

"I was angry, Ann."

She took his hand in both of hers. "We both have been. But it's all over now. That's why I came to the apartment complex last night. Bryant is gone." She waited for Morgan to reassure her that her problem was gone too, but he didn't. "What about Lara?"

"That's what I wanted to talk to you about last night before I got called away."

Annie let go of his hand, but he wouldn't release her. He gently squeezed her fingers.

The nurse walked into the room. "Well, good morning, Mr. Morgan. How are we feeling today?"

"Like we got run over last night. But I'll live."

"Well the doctor didn't find any signs of concussion. And now that you've had a good night's sleep, do you feel up to eating?"

"A little smoke inhalation never got in my way before."

"I hope waffles are okay. That's all they've got left this morning."

"More than okay."

The nurse paused, smiling at him. "I'll tell the kitchen."

"I still need to talk to you," Morgan said when she'd gone, "but it will have to wait." He started to get out of bed.

"Where do you think you're going? You can't get out of bed yet. The nurse is bringing your breakfast."

"I've got to use the bathroom."

Annie smiled and got up to help him. He waved her away, of course.

"You are the worst patient."

When he returned, his trip taking a little longer than anticipated because of dizziness, he found his breakfast waiting for him on a teal green tray. He dug into the two pale, room temperature waffles with a fork, finding that impossible. They smelled great, but after pouring maple syrup over them to soften them up, he found that they'd vulcanized into skeet disks. He ate them anyway, folding them in half and shoving them into his mouth like tacos.

Annie had never seen him eat syrup before let alone anything lacking whole grain. He washed the waffles down with an entire glass of orange juice and ate both sausage links on his tray.

"How was it?" She grinned.

"Microwaved food never tasted so good."

Annie looked away and bit her lower lip.

"I can tell something's wrong. Want to talk about your mother?"

Annie nodded.

"I know you've been trying to work out how she died, but have you considered that it was just her time?"

"No, because it wasn't. There are too many unanswered questions. My mother's friends are lying to me. Sarah Greis is dead, murdered. Her condominium emptied."

"None of that has anything to do with your mother. She died of natural causes."

"That's what we're supposed to think."

"Annie, I was hoping that if things got better between us, you'd be able to leave this behind you."

"And if I can't?"

Morgan looked down. The words he didn't say spoke louder than anything he could've. "You need to move on with your grief, for us."

"How can I? Someone wanted my mother dead."

"But you can't prove anything."

"I know." Annie hung her head.

"There's more, isn't there, something you haven't told me?"

She didn't know how Morgan always did it, always read her mind when she didn't want him to. She still had the puppies to find and couldn't possibly bother Morgan with that right now. "I've got to go out for a while, but I'll be back as soon as possible."

Morgan archcd a brow. "Now?"

"It's nothing, Morgan. It will just take me a little

while, and I'll come right back." She picked up her purse's strap.

He continued to watch her, not speaking.

She stood. "I don't want to bother you with it. I've just got something I have to do."

"Alone? Okay. Just tell me what it is you've got to do."

She hesitated.

"Uh, oh. I'm starting to feel a little woozy." He leaned back onto the bed pillows.

Annie's face whitened. "It's okay, Morgan. I'll call the nurse."

He grinned and looked at her from the corner of his half-closed eye.

"You! How could you scare me like that?"

He chuckled. "Tell me."

"I don't want to bother you with it. You need your rest."

"And you can depend on me."

"I know. It's the puppies. I've got to find them."

"Well, since puppies that small can't get up and walk away on their own, how did they get out?"

"Don't be angry." She took an audible breath and scrunched up her face. "Bryant."

Morgan sat up, his eyes sparking fire.

"This is why I didn't tell you. You shouldn't be upset."

"You let me worry about that."

"Morgan, I really need to go. I'll be back as soon as I can. I promise."

"We're not doing that anymore, you leaving, me leaving. I'm your husband, dammit. That means a whole hell of a lot to me. So from now on, we're more than husband and wife, we're partners. Where I go, you go. Where you go, I go." Morgan got up, reaching for his clothes which weren't there.

"They had to cut your jeans and t-shirt off in the ambulance."

"I knew that." Morgan cursed. "Go home. Get me some clothes. I'll be right here waiting. And if you're not back in twenty minutes, I'm coming for you like this." He pulled back the sheet, revealing his muscular thighs beneath the hospital gown, and Annie felt a surge of desire for this man come over her, a feeling she had greatly missed.

In record time, Annie returned to the sterile-smelling hall of the hospital. In the fifteen minutes she'd been gone, Morgan had been checked out and cleared to go home.

"The doctor says you have to take it easy for a few days."

Morgan grunted as he watched her with hungry eyes walk into the room. Without looking away from her, he pulled on the fresh change of underclothes and blue jeans she'd brought. He'd also showered while she'd been gone because water still clung to the tips of his hair as he slid the white polo over his head.

Still the sensation of relief stayed with her as she watched him dress; she hadn't lost him. He'd come out of this more determined as had she. He was going to be okay. He had his boots laced and his hand on her back, leading her to the door.

He slid behind the wheel of her Landcruiser like he hadn't just arrived there last night unconscious. He caught her watching him. "Don't worry, Ann. We'll get the puppies back."

She smiled. "It's not that." She looked down at her hands folded neatly in her lap. "It's," she took a deep breath, "I'm just so glad that you're okay."

He gently squeezed her hand. "Are we okay?"

Annie looked out the passenger window as they passed the hospital exit sign. There were too many more things she needed him to understand, too many to say right now. "I'm not sure."

"I am."

Annie tried to smile, but it faltered.

He let go of her hand. "Well, before we do anything else, if I'm going to be any good to you, I need some real food in my stomach."

She laughed now. Morgan was definitely going to be okay.

They breezed through the drive through line at Chickfila and as promised, he drove and ate simultaneously, so they were headed away from the restaurant in no time. Morgan said he felt much better after getting some protein into his system.

"So, where should we start? His house?" Morgan nearly choked on the last words, the last place on Earth he'd ever willingly go.

"I don't think he would've taken the puppies to his house."

As much as her heart resisted it, she could do nothing now short of trying to find Bryant, but she had no idea how long he'd been gone or what direction he went. Bryant had to have location services turned on so that his phone could use the same tracking that Morgan had on his phone. If Bryant had the ability to track from his phone, she could find him.

She turned on the app Morgan had installed with no trouble. In her contacts list, she found Bryant. Then like magic, a map appeared and a list of addresses, all places Bryant had been recently. Her house was there near the top. Above her house in the list was 1111 Ocean Boulevard, her mother's condominium address. And at the top of the list was the airport. She sighed in relief; Bryant had gone back to Italy.

"I know where the puppies are," she said.

"Where?"

"For some reason," she paused to look at Morgan, "Bryant must have taken them to Sunny Pines."

Morgan drove his truck as fast as he could without putting them in any further danger. Within minutes, they pulled into the condominium's parking lot. Annie jumped out of the truck, snatching up her purse from the seat, her phone inside it. Morgan jumped out behind her.

The front office door was locked. She sprinted to the back of the building, Morgan following right behind. Around the corner, in the humid breeze, she caught the boozy whiff of overripe bananas and heard the distant whimpering of puppies. She cupped her hands around her face and peered through the window. "No one's inside."

Sarah Greis' back yard gate, which butted up to the office building's fence, was locked. She tried to look through the slats in the privacy fence. "I can't see a thing."

Morgan knelt down on the grass beside her.

"Here," he said, holding her hand and pulling her foot to rest on his knee, "stand up."

She held her breath and lifted herself, looking over the fence, praying the puppies were there. The first thing she noticed was the box, the one she'd packed up her office with just days ago. "They're back here." She gasped. A chain link pen held many more than just her puppies, all whimpering. "There's more of them back here. But I don't see a mother dog. These can't all be from the same litter."

"I'll call the police," Morgan said.

"First, help me climb over. I want to get our puppies out."

"I don't know, Ann. It's pretty high. Let me do it."

"I'll do it. Give me a boost." Annie turned her back to Morgan and he placed both palms on her bottom.

"Be careful," he said, pushing slowly until her waist cleared the top of the fence. "Put your foot on the horizontal board then jump down."

Annie did, landing with a thud on the grass. Her purse slid from her shoulder and hit the ground. Moonlight glinted off the pearl handled revolver she'd taken from her mother's condo.

She ran to the puppies, all five of Glenda's babies tucked safely inside the box she recognized. She let go of the breath she'd held; they were okay.

The sliding glass door at the back of Sarah's condo creaked. The glass rippled and swayed in the moonlight. Someone stepped out of the shadows. Annie's heart raced and she silently knelt for the revolver, holding it out in front of her with both hands as she'd learned in the CWP class she'd taken with Morgan.

"Annie!" Betty Vitkevich sounded just as shocked to see her there as she was to see Betty. "What are you doing here?"

Annie took a breath, dropping the gun to her side. "I was just about to ask you the same thing."

"After you and I talked, I got worried about Sarah. I wanted to look for a number I could call her son in Michigan to find out how she is."

"Sarah's not in Michigan." Morgan landed inside the fence. "She's dead."

"How do you know that?"

"Morgan's a firefighter. *He* pulled her body out of that mill fire."

Betty's hand flew to her chest.

"You didn't know?"

"I," Betty stammered, "she was my best friend."

"If Sarah was your best friend," Morgan said, "then why did you let that happen to her?"

"I haven't seen her in months. I thought all this time she was with her son." Betty hung her head.

"What is all of this?" Annie said.

At least a dozen puppies were crammed into a metal run that took up the length of the twelve by twelve-foot yard.

"This is the investor's club's mess."

"What do you mean?"

"I mean that every month, we'd sell a new litter of puppies for cash. Pass them off as pure bred, no one seemed to question it, and invest the money."

"You all lived in the nicest condominiums in St. Michaels. It's not like you were broke. Why were you even doing this?"

"None of us had any savings to speak of, and we were looking at having to move in with our kids."

"Did you get any of the money from my mother to finance this?"

"I did. We all did. But she didn't know that's what the money was for."

"I see." That explained the notations in her mother's checkbook register. "You all lied to her that she was helping you pay for things you couldn't afford, like violin lessons for your grandchildren."

"Yes, she was the only one with any money. Her business. She was making money hand over fist."

"You assumed that because she had a successful business she had money to throw around?" Morgan said.

"Well, yes. Didn't she?"

Annie didn't answer. "When you started making money from the puppies, didn't my mother start to wonder where it came from?"

"Your mother had no way of knowing what was going on. We didn't tell Stella any of it. She wouldn't have gone along with it anyway. We lied to her that the money we made was from our lottery winnings. Oh, I hated lying to her. She was such a generous soul; she would've done anything for anyone. So we just kept up the charade to hide what was really going on."

"Who is the mother to all of these puppies?"

"My dog, Glenda."

Annie's mouth fell open. *Good thing you didn't get your hands back on her. Her life at least ended peacefully.* "How were you doing this?"

"Nancy and Henry wanted me because of my job at the pet store. I could bring the puppies in and sell them. That was the original plan, but the store wanted a big cut. So we decided to sell online."

"Since Henry Dekaretry obviously knew the whole time you had a dog, what was the real reason he kicked you out of your condo?"

"When Glenda ran off, I got cold feet. I went looking for her at the Humane Society. She wasn't there, but I thought I recognized some of her puppies from previous litters. They looked just like her. I found an employee spraying out an empty cage and asked him about them. He said they'd been getting a lot of dogs turned in recently from people who'd said they thought they'd bought a pure bred, only to find later that they weren't. He said they were looking into it with the sheriff's department. I didn't want to go to jail. I told Henry Dekaretry that. He said I was being an irrational old woman and told me to keep my mouth shut."

"So, they had to get rid of you so you wouldn't try to stop them."

"They wanted to keep selling Glenda's puppies. I wouldn't let them."

Annie's heart broke for poor Glenda, giving birth to a litter of her puppies only to have to repeat the process over again.

"Why didn't you tell me before about the puppies in Sarah's backyard?" Annie said. "I could've done something about it without Henry or Nancy finding out."

"I didn't want to get Sarah kicked out of her condo too." Betty put her face in her hands. "Sarah would never have gone along with what they wanted. She had too good a heart."

"Well, she may have died because she didn't want to go along with them."

Betty looked up at Annie wide-eyed. She backed into a rusted metal patio chair and sat down hard. "I knew she was strapped for money like the rest of us, but I never thought she'd kill for it."

"Who? Nancy? Did Nancy kill Sarah?"

The older woman stared absently at the far end of the yard where the privacy fence cut a square in the Zoysia grass. "Her husband of only two years went to prison for embezzling. I'm not supposed to know that. No one is. I guess your mother heard about it from Nancy," Betty shrugged, "I don't know. She must've accidentally let it slip."

Is that why my mother is dead too?

The glass door behind Betty slid open. Henry Dekaretry and Nancy Carlucci stepped out. As soon as they laid eyes on Morgan, standing behind Annie, they turned and ran.

"Wait!" Annie shouted.

"Don't worry," Morgan said. "They won't get far. The police are already here."

Sirens wailed in the distance, coming closer.

Morgan stood guard at the sliding glass door in case Henry came back to defend his money maker.

A St. Michael's uniformed police officer appeared at Sarah's patio door. His deep voice mingled with Morgan's, but Annie took no notice. She sat down cross-legged inside the pen, counting puppies, letting the older ones crawl into her lap to sniff and lick her fingers. "Fourteen, fifteen..."

"Sixteen in all," she said to Morgan who stood over her now. "And they're all going to need homes. They'll have to come home with us, just until we can find homes for them."

Morgan shook his head, grinning down at his wife covered in wagging tails and flopping ears. "Theresa will be so pleased."

Annie reached up, taking his proffered hand and flung her arms around his neck as he lifted her to her feet.

He placed sixteen puppies of various sizes, but all resembling their mother, inside the back seat of the truck. He placed theirs beside Annie so that she could marvel at their little faces as they drove.

As she smiled down at them, she gasped. "How did Bryant know to drop the puppies here?"

Morgan shrugged. "You said Bryant had tracking on his cell phone. If he tracked you or me here, he might have stumbled upon them by accident. But he already knew your mother lived here."

"True, but she never liked him. He never came here."

"Good. I always did like your mother."

Annie burst into laughter.

"Plus he's obviously got a sick mind."

"Yeah, I know how to pick 'em, don't I?"

Morgan slid his hand behind her hair, cupping her neck and giving her a sidelong glance. "You sure do. But you didn't pick Bryant. You picked me."

Annie burst through the front door and rushed to the kitchen where Theresa lay with her head on her bed, mourning the loss of her puppies.

Morgan carried the box into the house behind Annie, carefully setting it down in front of the mother dog and stepped back.

Theresa whimpered when she saw her puppies.

"Everything's okay now," Annie said as much to herself as to Theresa.

Theresa must have agreed because she wagged and sniffed them all, drooling as she did.

Annie squatted beside the little family as the mother dog prodded each baby with her nose, checking them to be sure for herself that they were okay. Mother and babies all safe and back in their home next to the refrigerator, Theresa washed them in turns, removing from their little bodies the scent of the man who'd taken them.

Annie watched in awe. "I hope I'm as good a mother someday as you are."

Theresa must not have heard because she didn't stop her washing, loving her adopted puppies the way only a mother does.

"We're a family now," Annie smiled up at Morgan, who stood behind her, "a big one."

Morgan chuckled. "I'm glad."

"So," Annie chewed her bottom lip, "what was it that you wanted to talk to me about before?"

Morgan's expression hardened. "Before I got called away to the fire—wait a second, I've got a question for you about that. What were you doing there in the first place?"

"Looking for you. I had something I needed to tell you too."

"And what was that?"

Annie stood and faced him. "That I've tried to do things all by myself for too long. I've tried to be independent because that's what I thought you wanted from me. You handle all of your problems by yourself, never ask me for help. I tried to do the same. Trouble is, I don't want to. What's the use of being married if we can't depend on each other?"

Morgan chuckled softly. "Now, that's exactly what I wanted to say to you. Before I left for the fire, I wanted to tell you that I know you wanted to pay for a honeymoon with your savings."

"I forgot all about it," Annie said, practically running to the kitchen drawer where she'd left it.

"Forgot what?"

"The wedding gift my mother gave us."

She ripped open the envelope now, sure there was money inside. And she was right. Inside was a bond for five thousand dollars. Annie's heart squeezed. She held the paper against her chest. Money her mother could have used when she was alive, she'd given them as a gift. Tears welled in her eyes. "Now we can take our honeymoon."

"No." Morgan shook his head, seeing what the gift meant to Annie. "Let me pay for it. Put that check in savings to repay you for your mother's funeral expenses. She would've wanted you to. Business has been really good lately. I can afford it."

At the mere mention of business, Annie crossed her arms over her abdomen and looked out the window.

"Ann, stay with me here. Lara isn't in the picture. She never was." He reached for Annie's chin, forcing her to look at his face. "She's not you."

Annie looked into Morgan's deep blue eyes. His irises, surrounded by red blood vessels, shone even brighter than usual. "Morgan, I'm so sorry I ever made you feel about Bryant the way I feel towards Lara. I've never had feelings for him the way I have for you. He was never more than a friend. And not even that anymore. Things are different now. I can't be friends with him and be the wife I want to be to you."

"Give me a second chance to be the husband I should've been to you."

"Of course. There's no question."

Morgan touched her cheeks with his fingertips and brought her face to his. He kissed her, long and deep. She melted in his hands. And when he lifted his head, he'd stolen her breath.

"Well, then, since we're starting fresh here," Morgan said, "I've got a proposal for you."

"Oh, yeah?" Annie said, still a little light-headed from the kiss. "What is it?"

"That honeymoon we never took."

"Yes." She bit her lower lip.

"There are five fire departments in Hawaii that I want to meet with."

Annie wrinkled her nose. "Aren't there any fire departments in North Carolina you want to meet with?"

"I thought you'd say that." Morgan chuckled. "I'm sure we could find some."

"Really?"

"Let's go, Ann."

She leaned forward and wrapped her arms around the back of his neck, hugging him.

"And I want you to come with me on sales trips from now on. You're not teaching anymore, and I could use a brain like yours for figures. Be my business partner. What do you say?"

Annie kissed him. "You've got it."

"Great." He hesitated. "Just so you know, I don't think you're crazy."

Annie looked down at her hands. "You heard all that?"

"I was asleep, not in a coma."

"I'm sorry. I was crazed with worry."

"Don't be. She's just projecting."

"You're smart, you know that?"

"For a fireman?"

"For a lot of reasons. First, you married me." Annie smiled.

He took her hand. "You're the most honest, forthright person I've ever known. No one could question your integrity. And don't let my mother's problems define you. You're your own woman. And if my mother can't see that, that's her loss. I was a fool to even think there was anything between you and Bryant. You're way too honest. You'd have told me all about it long before it ever became anything."

"And don't you forget it."

Morgan squeezed Annie's hand. His expression fell. "Annie, we almost didn't make it back here."

"You mean you didn't." She tried teasing him but found she couldn't. She wasn't ready. Her smile fell too. "Eddie said he pulled you out of that fire."

Morgan nodded, but said nothing. Too soon. He would talk about it one day.

"But we're here now," she said. "That's all that

matters."

"Yeah, but look how far we pushed each other away. I almost let Lara suck me in because I thought you didn't need me anymore. I thought Bryant had a hold on you and I couldn't get you back from him."

"No one could ever take me away from you, Morgan."

He removed a piece of paper from his pocket.

"What's this?" she said.

"My phone code."

"Zero five two seven."

"Our anniversary."

"May twenty-seventh." Annie smiled.

"Next week, North Carolina. Just the two of us."

"Yes."

"I love you, Annie Morgan."

"I love you too, Chance Morgan."

Neither of them spoke for several moments. When he finally did, his deep voice sounded thick. "I've always been faithful to you, Annie, never even considered another woman. You're all I've ever wanted and everything I need."

He reached for her hand, guiding her along with him up the creaky stairs. Once inside their bedroom, standing behind her as she reached for the light switch, he stopped her hand. "Leave the lights on." He brushed her hair away from her neck where he kissed each and every scar. With strong hands he gently massaged her shoulders. She didn't stiffen or try to pull away from him this time as she'd done so many times in the past. She let him pull her against his chest.

His body behind her touched the top of her

shoulders down to her calves. She sighed. Something inside the two of them had shifted, as if they were no longer the same two people they had been. A new day had dawned in their relationship that brought with it the hope and promise of a new life. She didn't have to remind herself not to worry that their love-making should produce a son or a daughter, she didn't have to try to force her body to relax and enjoy. All of these things happened of their own volition as if not only had their relationship altered its course, but so had she. Her thoughts were different now.

Morgan's deep voice brought her mind back to the present moment. "Annie, is everything okay?"

She smiled and leaned her head back onto his chest. "I was just thinking how much I'm enjoying this."

He murmured deep in his throat, a sound that conveyed his own pleasure. He plunged his hands down the front of her chest, pulling and plucking open her blouse. His hands on her shoulders, he turned her around to meet his eyes, her chest bare. His expression intent, he cupped her cheeks in his strong hands and bent to kiss her lips. The kiss began softly as if he were afraid to rush her, afraid that old fears would resurface and take her away from him once again. But her feet did not move; she didn't turn away. She let his hands explore the tender softness of her chest and abdomen. Placing a hand on either side of her waist, he lifted her to meet his kisses that became more and more insistent with each passing second. Strong arms lifted her off her feet, cupping her buttocks with both hands. Instinctively, she wrapped her legs around his waist, pulling herself closer to him.

And as she did, he chuckled deep in his chest. "That's it," he said slowly. "Enjoy all of it."

She smiled as he kissed her lips, her cheeks, her neck. He walked to the bed, carrying her, where he placed her down gently in the center. He followed her, kissing as he bent over her. Then with her arms around his neck, she pulled him off his feet so that he landed with a groan of delight on top of her. Every inch of her reveled in the feel of his masculine body. "I've missed you." She sighed.

"I've missed you too, Annie." His voice was a reverent whisper as his lips explored the tender swell of her breasts. "Never let me go again."

Holding onto her, he rolled with her now so that she lay on top of him, facing him.

"I won't," she said, smiling. "I promise."

He pushed the blouse she still wore from her shoulders, revealing soft, supple skin. He nuzzled her breasts still covered by her bra. "Take it off."

She did, removing the lace that hid her treasures.

As he watched her fingers push away the straps from her shoulders, he sucked in a breath. "You're so beautiful, Ann. Every time I see your naked body, it's like the first time."

She smiled and tugged at the hem of his polo, trying to pull it off of him. With one hand, he pulled the shirt over his head, revealing the body she had memorized. She ran her hands over his muscled chest and the flat plane of his abdomen where soft hairs curled and tickled her palms.

He smiled, reveling in the softness of her touch. His body never ceased to react to hers. The more she touched, the more he needed her. His body rose up, demanding the sweet relief only Annie could give him.

She reached for the button of his jeans and he covered her hand with his.

"Let me." He could not wait for her small hands to find their way. He had to rid himself of the barrier between them quickly; he didn't have a choice. An urgency deep inside him he had not known before drove him. He wanted her in a way that went beyond hunger.

Need. Pure and simple.

With all clothing completely out of their way, he pulled her back to him. He guided her hips to his so that they were perfectly fitted together.

She gasped as he filled her.

He held her gently, his hands about her waist and watched her with hungry eyes as she began to move on top of him. But as his hunger grew, so did his need for her body beneath his. He lifted her and placed her gently beneath him. He found her innermost secrets once more, this time not only aware of his body's insistent desire but in awe of her body and the power it held over him, the power to bring him to his knees.

Morgan whispered Annie's name as he entered her once more.

And as they held each other in the ancient rhythm of their love-making, as old as the tide, their bodies cried out in simultaneous completion. For they were made complete when they were together, two bodies made stronger by their bond of love, two souls irrevocably bound together in time and space, destined to love and live forever.

Wearing just her bathrobe, Annie left Morgan asleep in their bed. She tiptoed into the office. In her hand was the elephant statue she had kept from her mother's condo. "I still don't know what happened to you, mother. Or why. But I will find out."

"An elephant never forgets," she could hear her mother say.

"I promise." Annie placed the elephant on her make-shift desk next to her laptop.

She would never forget, not after what she'd just been through. She didn't need to lose her husband too to remember how much she needed him. They would be alright from now on.

Theresa had been right after all. Coming to them had been just what she'd promised—family.

Annie left the room with a new sense of peace. Her chest didn't ache the way it always had, longing for the child they hadn't conceived.

She tiptoed back into their bedroom.

Morgan slowly opened his eyes and smiled a sleepy smile.

"Let's go swimming." She grasped his hand.

"Right now?"

She nodded, smiling.

He stepped into his jeans and followed her outside barefooted to where the grass faded into sand, rising up to dunes.

The moon illuminated the ripples on the water's glassy surface and the horizon that stretched out before then now was limitless, open, waiting for them.

About the Author

Tina Proffitt is the author of romance novels set in small, Southern towns, one historical fiction romance, and one non-fiction book about past lives with present animals, mother to two life-long home-schooled teenagers, and wife to her best friend and hero.

She holds a Bachelor of Science in Education Degree with a concentration in Math from the University of South Carolina and loves to read all things medieval, mysterious, and mystical.

She can be reached at her website.
Blogger: *Recipes from a Writer*
Goodreads
Pinterest
Facebook: Tina Proffitt Author Page
Twitter: @tina_proffitt
Instagram: tina_proffitt

A Note from the Author

The hardest part about being married to a career firefighter for the past two decades has been going to bed and waking up alone, something I think Annie can relate to. But all this time alone taught me a thing or two about fear. One of them is not to focus on it every time he leaves for work. It doesn't help. And if I'd let it, it would have taken over my life. The other is to do the thing that scares you.

Over the years, every time I started writing a new romance, I would think, will this be the one I put all of my experiences as the wife of a firefighter to work for me? Will I write this one about a sexy firefighter hero? And for nearly a decade, without a conscious decision on my part, I haven't. There was always another story more pressing to tell. Then when the subject of retirement came up, as if the clouds parted above, I said, my next book will be about a firefighter and his wife. All of a sudden, I knew I could write that book, put my scariest fears, my darkest moments, and my deepest pride into a hero who did what my husband had done for the past twenty-five years.

It's possible that I'd only been kidding myself that I had been brave by not worrying about him every time he left for another twenty-four-hour shift or an off-duty call, because something had held me back from writing this story, from thinking about it too much, from considering it from my own point of view. But I'm so glad I finally did!

-*Tina*

Thank you for supporting independent publishing!

Please Rate/Review this book on Amazon or Goodreads. Thank you!

Novels by Tina Proffitt:

First Forever: Fredericksburg County Series Book 1
Second Chances: Fredericksburg County Series Book 2
Third Time's the Charm: Fredericksburg County Series Book 3
A Sprinkle of Magick
Shadow Walker
Parlor Favors
The Almoner's Tale
Red Nobody
Ten for a Bird
Event Horizon: Chances Are Series Book 1
Heart of Gold: Chances Are Series Book 2
More books in this series coming soon!

Printed in Great Britain
by Amazon